THE SINGULAR CASE OF THE MULTIPLE DEAD

By the same author

ILL MET BY A FISH SHOP ON GEORGE STREET

THE CRIMSON MADNESS OF LITTLE DOOM

NIGHT'S EVIL

THE GIRL NOBODY KNOWS

UNTIMELY RIPPED

SÉANCE

THE SINGULAR CASE OF THE MULTIPLE DEAD

MARK McSHANE

KING CRIME

HODDER AND STOUGHTON

First printed in Great Britain 1970

SBN 340 12886 0

Reproduced from the original setting by arrangement with G. P. Putnam's Sons New York

Printed in Great Britain for Hodder and Stoughton Limited, St. Paul's House, Warwick Lane, London, E.C.4, by Lowe & Brydone (Printers) Ltd., London

THE SINGULAR CASE
OF THE MULTIPLE DEAD

one

Mr. Jem Gate cupped his hand lovingly around the angel's breast. There was no doubt about it, he thought: He was good with breasts. A genuine breast man, in fact. Others could brag about their faces and their hips and their calf muscles or whatever, but when it came to the old tit work, there was no one better than Jem Gate. He never went too far. He knew when to stop. He always left the nipple just that little bit underdefined, hardly there at all, respectable.

Jem stood back to look at the statue, one hand clasping chisel and hammer, the other intent on rubbing together its forefinger and thumb. He looked over the head and shoulders and the two shapeless blocks which would become wings until, aided by the sifting thumb and finger, he found what he wanted—a word to replace "respectable," for which in this context he had no liking, it smacking too much of the artisan, too little of the artist.

Decent. That was the word. Decent. His breasts would offend no one. You could take them anywhere. You could let them be looked at by the kiddies. You would never be ashamed to stand up and say, "Yes, them's mine."

Navels, now. Take navels. They were something else. No matter what you did with navels they always looked suggestive. The best way was the Gate way. Cover them with a bit of raiment, a forearm, the odd scroll of parchment, a lyre. No problem. Nothing too difficult to make. And why? Why? Need anyone ask? Well, if anyone need, he wasn't merely a stonemason, that's why. He was a sculptor.

Jem Gate's thought chain ended triumphantly, on a high note. It could go no further. It had reached the ultimate.

Giving the angel's breast a final pat, in whose pride was mingled a pinch of pity for its inability to reach the same heights as himself, Jem turned and wended across his yard through the statues and columns and headstones. It was time for him to leave; time for him to attend the extraordinary meeting of Bloomsbury Group Junior.

Jem felt a twinge of excitement. Soon he would be within the magic circle. He would be associating with soul mates, with artists and intellectuals. He would be at home.

His excitement turned to gratitude. Lady Severn and the others had changed his life. They formed an oasis in this workaday world. For as long as he could remember he had dreamed of mixing with his own kind, able to say what he thought and felt instead of choking everything back for fear of being laughed at. That this back choking had led him to become in time something less than glib was, he felt, unimportant. Speech was not necessary. Only the ambience mattered. He was an aesthete among aesthetes. He was breathing air that was drenched with creativity.

Jem stepped inside the cottage which formed his home and office, a chaos of household and business equipment, an atmosphere redolent with grinding oil and kippers. Centrally stood a dusty rolltop desk, at which Jem pointed accusingly in thinking: That's where it happened. No more than six months ago. Waited there for a bit of marble to be polished, she did. Lady Severn. Nice as you like. No side. Then what does she up and say?—after looking all the time at the latest work, cherubs paired on column fluted with heels winged—what does she say?

"Mr. Gate, my dear Mr. Gate, do you realize that you are an artist?"

Overwhelmed, he had opened his heart. He had said, "Yes."

Everything began from that. He had been introduced to and become a member of the small elite group which met regularly in Lady Severn's salon to listen to music, read poetry or plays, and discuss Things That Matter. To Jem Gate's life had been added another dimension.

If he had a regret, it was that Bloomsbury Group Junior had no political overtones (had, indeed, a flavor strongly apolitical), because he felt that as a citizen of his community he should be more involved and do things such as, for instance, vote. In fact he had been considering putting this remissness to rights by listening regularly to speeches on the television when Lady Severn appeared. Now he denied himself politics. His patroness, he was certain, would be disappointed in him, which must never happen.

Jem went into his bedroom, a place as untidy as the office-parlor and with some overspill of its chattels—samples of stone, half-moons of marble, and a large dining table which, from shortage of space, had been stood on the bed to create a dwarf four-poster; a sinister refugee from Poe, caught in the act. One of the room's damp-happy walls was papered with slips of photogravure, all curled in various stages of rejection and all featuring sculptures.

Despite the mildness of the April afternoon, Jem's home was cold; he hurried as he changed from coveralls to a heavy blue serge, double of breast, raised of seam, uncompromising of nature.

Jem Gate was not one of those who felt the outer man should match the inner. His only feelings attached to the outer were those of sensation. He was unconcerned about his appearance, apart from rudimentary neatness. He was even vague as to how he appeared. He knew, more or less, that he was short and broad, had black curly hair, dark eyes, and sound teeth. Nothing was known to him of the attractive steadiness of his gaze, his strong jaw, the threat in his bullock neck and hands of blacksmith girth, the warming eye lines of kindness. If he thought about age at all, it was merely insofar as being proud that he had attained a decent, solid forty-five, was no longer a flighty lad.

Dressed now, boots dusted off, lariated with a black tie, which after twelve years he still wore to celebrate the passing of the babe whose birth had caused his wife's death, Jem went outside and made for a corner of the yard to give his sole employee detailed instructions. He liked to keep a firm hand on the running of his business.

The stringy apprentice was leaning on a headstone, finished but unsold, a remainder that was available at a special rate to anyone who might wish to announce that a Minnie Cleg had left the arms of her harold Husband. He was not a very good apprentice.

"Well," said Jem.

The stringy man nodded. "You're off now, so I'd better keep my eye on things and not dawdle, also lock up securely and leave the burglar light on when I go, hadn't I? And I mustn't forget to tell that woman if she comes back that you'll take the job, must I?"

"Yes," Jem said. "Afternoon."

Out on the glum suburban street he climbed into his pickup, an ancient Rolls Royce which had been cut down in haphazard fashion from a hearse to a truck. He drove off.

His goal in mind, he wondered again why the Group was being called to an extraordinary meeting, and again he replied to the wonder, quickly, sternly, that no, of course, it had nothing to do with himself, there was absolutely no reason why the others should suddenly want to hand him the blackball because his work was tainted with commercialism. They knew he was going to turn pure when he could afford to. Besides, Lady Severn would stand for no such nonsense. She was his patron and mentor and friend. She would do anything for him, and he would do anything for her, only double. She had brought him his first happiness in twelve years. She was the finest woman in the world.

"Right," he said firmly.

* * *

Bloomsbury. A street of red-brick houses blamed on Queen Anne. The long, unbroken façades hid a strife dating back to the flat makers' rape. The tenants didn't like the flats, getting only a share of the fading glamour, the flats felt awkward in the houses, like sensitive gate-crashers fearful of being challenged, and the houses were affronted by the files of parked cars all of which, as if anachronism were not a serious enough complaint, looked to be on the point of rising in a mass copulation.

Only one resident ever gazed out into the street with anything like pleasure. Lady Severn. Even after a tenancy of fourteen months, she still felt stirred to be here in London, in Bloomsbury, in her own elegant apartment.

She was gazing out now dreamily as, with little finger extended in a genteel tine, she prodded about in a nostril. So much history, she was thinking. So many things had happened here. It needed no great effort of the imagination to picture Lytton Strachey out there leaning gracefully on one of the parking meters.

Turning to face the room, Madge Severn made a mental note to try and get a print of a Strachey painting.

The room was large and had style. All the color schemes, textiles, rugs, mock-Anne furniture, and modern pieces blended beautifully. It was the work of a previous tenant.

The eye of Lady Severn came to rest on the room's only other occupant, a young man of startling good looks. Olive-skinned, black of wavy hair and eye, wearing an impeccably cut suit, the young man stood staring into space, looking as unreal and vaguely horrific as a window dummy.

Adonis, thought Madge, where are you now?

In spirit, Tony Zero was where he stood in the flesh, except that the flat had been transported to his home village in Italy, becoming his own property on the way and settled above a garage which held seventeen white convertibles.

Madge smiled. She was proud of Tony. He had been her first acquisition when she had set about the task of surrounding herself with the right people in founding her salon.

She had met him at a night-school drawing class, which she had attended once only, eschewing further lessons because it was quite, quite obvious that the other students and teachers were totally lacking in soul. Tony had been the model. She had taken him out for a drink afterward and despite his ultra-poor English had learned that he had been in England two years, worked as a chef's aid, with the odd-modeling job, wanted to be a designer, and would charge only five pounds if she desired to go to bed with him. This last notion charmed and flattered Lady Severn. She declined apologetically. He said he was very clean. She pointed out that she was old enough to be his grandmother. He offered to wear a beard. She explained that she had lost interest in sex. Tearfully sympathetic, he asked why she didn't poison herself.

They became firm, fond friends, though Tony never entirely gave up the hope that someday their relationship would rise to a more profound, commercial level.

"Penny for them, Tony?"

At the mention of coin Tony Zero became alert. "Please?"

"Never mind," said Madge, who did not always feel up to the strain of explanation. "Sit down, dear. The others will be here soon."

Tony sat. "Yes, it is."

A penny would have been too great a sum for Tony's thoughts, since he had not been thinking, having returned from Italy when he sensed himself being stared at. He had merely been keeping still, wishing to afford the watcher every assistance. He was a kind person. He accepted the work as part of the trial of being beautiful.

Lady Severn turned back to the window, and Tony was able to reverse their recent roles. He examined the tall stately figure in a greenish tweed suit and with a face he always thought of as Swedish modern.

To most other people, the face of angles and arches was aristocratic; at the least landed gentry. The bright blue eyes might have conquered William or quailed a serf, scorched a Roundhead or obliged a noble, twinkled smile from a cowgirl's baby, or frozen the host belowstairs. The upper lip was long and stiff. The nose had nostrils whose smallness could only have been caused by ancestors' refusal to inhale of the great unwashed. The chin spoke of fighting on beaches and landing grounds, in fields and streets and hills, of never surrendering. The whole had long been dedicated to a public show of serenity.

No one would guess that Madge Severn's pre-London life had been a series of disappointments, sixty years of being let down. Daddy, unforgivably, had been a vicar, not an Indian scout, and Mama had steadfastly refused to climb trees or go on the stage or smoke cigarettes. Little friends had been beastly in asking at times to take over Madge's role as ringleader. God had been against her in every way, making her plain and pimply and causing the weather always to be wrong; at fifteen she wrote his name in her diary, drew a line through it, and had not given him a thought since. School had been a mess of pretty girls, teachers who insisted on doing things their own way, and examiners who failed her out of perversity. The deb year was a chaos of more pretty girls, dancing partners who were never in step, and dates too shy to try anything on. The man she wanted to marry foolishly chose someone else. The man she did marry had failed her in being unable to sire children—though the doctors, maddeningly, persisted in their silly belief that she was to blame. The queen had gone out of her way not to give Mr. Severn a knighthood, which he so obviously deserved for all his work on the village council and paying toward the erection of a new storage shed at the cricket club. And finally, the lawyers had let her down by getting Mr. Severn's will mixed up with someone else's and giving her much less than she had expected. She had been able to afford only a short nervous breakdown.

Afterward, however, there had been an improvement in people. Cutting old ties, assuming the title that was hers by right, she had come to London and started a new life among delightful Bohemians.

These new friends, mused Madge, would never be a disappointment. They were as fond of her as she was of them. Besides, their minds were always a million miles away from the here and now. Tony, for instance.

Shortening her vision Madge looked at instead of through the window, at the room's reflection. Tony sat like a statue. If Madge had ever seen someone whose mind was a million miles away from the here and now, it was Tony. She thought, On what do you cogitate, Adonis?

Tony's mind was on the other side of the room, on a bookcase. He was wondering why the author had none of her own books there, especially those said to be about Italian rivers and trees. (Tony had long ago reached the odd conclusion that his hostess was Gertrude Stein.)

He realized that Lady Severn had spoken, had put a question. Wrinkling his beautiful brow in the way he knew to be appealing, he looked toward her and asked for a repeat. She put the question again. Tony did a slow translation and found to his surprise that the essential verb was "murder."

Virginius Twyce was tall and thin. He was twenty-nine years of age. He wore spectacles with steel rims, a gray flannel suit with padded shoulders, shoes with the minimum of heel. He had red hair running thin, a redhead's freckled paleness, a sharp nose, and a nervous self-biting mouth.

As he stood on the corner of the street, his mouth was attacking itself bitterly. He couldn't decide whether to go on down to Lady Severn's or wait a little longer. He didn't want to be too early. On the other hand, if he dawdled here, some of the others might see him as they approached and he would look an idiot.

Teeth chaveling his bottom lip, Virginius fretted at the question of whether it was better to be too early or to look an idiot. He added a frown and a scouring of the hands.

Unable to find an answer, he chose the only way out, which he considered to be not without merit. He turned and ran off in the opposite direction.

Virginius Twyce was a professional worrier. He worried about losing his secretarial job, about anyone seeing his miserable bed-sitter, about outbreaks of flu in places he had never heard of, about the losers of sporting events he didn't understand, about some gold digger getting the impression he was rich and marrying him for his money and then being annoyed with him when she found out he was poor, about his outleaping hair, about loss of sleep through worry.

His main fester these days was that Bloomsbury Group Junior would discover he did not know *quite* as much about Georgian silver as he claimed. He did know a lot, but not that much; he was learning, but it was a slow business. He read books and catalogues and sneered on Portobello Road and on free days went to the class auction houses. It was through one of these last that he had met the Group.

He had been standing in Christie's, playing his game of pretending to bid, lifting a forefinger that was safely hidden in a pocket and scowling at rivals with his ears, when a man beside him gasped, "Twelve thousand guineas!"—which he quickly chased into gibberish with a blurt of coughing before swinging around and rushing out. Worried, Virginius followed, caught the man up, and told him not to worry, explaining that he had almost done the same thing himself many times.

They became friends on the spot. They were of a kind. Apart from age and main interest—Relentable Cease being sixty-odd and a composer—they had many things in common: bed-sitter, love of music and artifacts, flat feet, loneliness. Proudly Mr. Cease took his discovery along to Lady Severn's, a day Virginius had marked on his calendar in red crayon, writing which almost papably sobbed.

Virginius broke off his run and looked around haggardly for a policeman who might accost him and ask what had been his hurry. Catching a bus was a good story, he thought. What bus? Headed where? Virginius was panicking until he realized there was not a policeman in sight. Panting, he began to stroll back.

Yes, he thought, he would have to be careful at the meeting. Last week he had come close to saying something which would have clearly shown he was terribly weak on candlesticks. If the others realized . . . if they threw him out. . . .

It was unthinkable. Life would not be worth living. The Group had made him a new man. It had brought a beauty into his existence. How could he go on without the meetings, the brilliant conversation, the communing of creative and appreciative spirits, the theater outings, and the trips to the country? He just couldn't, that was all, and he wouldn't.

Virginius reached the fateful corner. He tugged down his jacket, adjusted his spectacles, had a good bite at both lips —and decided to wait awhile. He didn't want to be too early. On the other hand. . . .

Miss Minerva Droplet was excited. She had been excited ever since the floor manager had come to her counter (Remnants) and said frostily that she was wanted on the telephone. It was Mr. Cease, the Group's unofficial messenger. There was an emergency meeting. She had to be there. It was all frightfully mysterious and thrilling.

Minerva paused in her charge toward a box of earrings to clasp both hands to her heart, close her eyes, and cherish the thought, I am excited.

Minerva was a large girl of thirty. She had a bouncy body, leaping of buttock and breast, a head of tight blond curls, and a face that was pretty aside from its protruding blue eyes and its look of unoccupancy. All in all, she was a reflection of the watercolors she spent so much time on, which lined the walls of her flat: oversized and overstated, cute but vacuous.

After a period of some months, Miss Droplet had still not gotten over the shock of finding that Bloomsbury Group Junior, true *cognoscenti,* considered her paintings to be excellent, first-rate. Before, everyone had thought them worthless. Once, emboldened by a prelunch sherry, she had taken some pictures into a Bond Street gallery. The dealer had had a good laugh, thanked her for making his day, and pleaded to be told who had put her up to it. She realized now that the man was a Philistine, unable to recognize talent. The Group had brought her peace of mind.

Minerva was enthralled with her friends. Even without the subconscious gratitude she would have been enthralled. They were the very type she had always dreamed of knowing —dreams dismissed as foolish and romantic. She knew that she was mixing with the creative cream of the era. Someday their names would be household words. Someday there would be dozens of books and theses on them. Someday she would read things like "It was at Lady Severn's that I first met Minerva Droplet, the watercolorist." Or "Research has shown that the driving force of the famous clique was the beautiful Minerva." Or "It was after seeing Droplet's work at her fantastically successful one-man that my own painting began to improve."

She often embroidered these with ". . . the well-known Bond Street dealer, who shot himself at the Droplet one-man." Another favorite embroidery was "I count myself lucky that I was one of the special few there that day when Minerva announced her engagement to Mr. Fourpenny, the poet."

Drawing in a shriek of air to get her skirt fastened, Minerva wondered about the depth of her feeling for Mr. Fourpenny. Perhaps it was only that of the Group he was the most appropriate. Mr. Cease and Mr. Gate were too old; Virginius, poor dear, was too unattractive; and Tony, well, he was too everything.

Minerva flushed as she recalled the evening Tony had walked her home and offered five pounds if she would let him join her in bed. When she sweatily refused, he'd had the nerve to *reduce* his price, offering four pounds ten.

It was not that she was against sex, just against commercial sex. Venery went with love, and it was for love alone that she had in the past given herself to impetuous beaux, though admittedly not without resistance, murmuring "No" and "Oh, dear" while shifting limbs to facilitate garment removal and sighing "Never" while heeling off her shoes. However, she could say with pride that she had not been promiscuous. She had indulged in all only fifteen times, once with each of the fifteen men she had loved to desperation.

There had been no second time, because she refused it without marriage, and this the men had declined, obviously not bei .g mature enough.

Was Sid Fourpenny Mr. Right? In truth, Minerva was not frightfully concerned. It would of course be rather jolly to be engaged to a poet, but her big romance of the moment was with Bloomsbury Group Junior, and in any case Mr. Fourpenny had not yet progressed beyond wistful glances, being somewhat lacking in maturity, as well as a poet.

Minerva finished dressing, blundered out of the flat, and throbbed downstairs. Outside she halted with astonishment. There, at the curb, rakishly astride his motor-assisted bicycle, was none other than Mr. Fourpenny himself.

Minerva blushed, her eyes glared coyly, she used an intimate tone to cover the intervening two yards with a shout of "Good afternoon!"

"How do you do, Miss Droplet," said Mr. Fourpenny in his choked, poetic way. "I took the liberty of calling to pick you up."

"How kind, how thoughtful!"

"Not at all."

"Yes at all," Minerva said, pulping his hand. "Frightfully at all."

Mouth held, as always, like that of a ventriloquist, Sid Fourpenny oozed, "My pleasure. Hop on."

Minerva sat herself side-pillion. Roaring, the bike faltered forward. Who would ever guess that on this gallant machine sat a poet and a painter, thought Minerva. No one, came the answering thought, fighting back its disappointment.

True, Sid Fourpenny did not look like a poet. He looked like a pimp. Medium build, wiry, wearing clothes best described as sharp, he had a swarthy face of vicious features and a small mustache which, complemented by a slob of goo'd-down black hair, went more with the street corner than the attic.

The impression was not reliable. Sid was a respectable greengrocer from the respectable suburb of Enfield. Furthermore, he did have a feeling for poetry (he owned a volume of Robert W. Service and could quote whole lines from Antoine D'Arcy), a feeling which had increased tenfold since his becoming a member of the Group, though it was connected only indirectly with his joining.

Sid was a man of passion, a bird man, a constant seeker after tail, perpetually concerned with getting his end in. He had enjoyed the usual youthful successes, then had come the lean years. By the age of twenty-five, growing more soured- and sordid-looking every day, he had been reduced to wheedling the favors of an occasional housewife with extra weight in potatoes and the odd gift of a bunch of carrots. Reaching reluctantly for thirty, he was making out like a eunuch in a school for lesbians.

He had found some consolation in poetry, his liking for which had been something of a shock and which he had managed to hide from his mates at the billiard hall and pub. Yet curiously enough, one of his mates it was who gave him his idea for a change in tactics.

Over beers they had been discussing press reports of a Chelsea orgy. Sid grumbled that it sounded exaggerated. His friend told what he had been told by a cousin who sold art supplies, that these here artists and like that was sex mad, once you was in with them you couldn't go wrong, the birds would drop their drawers at the very sight of canvas or mention of Hamlet.

Sid was convinced. He himself had heard about this free-love lark. Why should he not cop for some of it? And as it happened, he had a plan that might get him "in."

"Young Poet wd like meet lady with similar interests" read the ad he placed in a newspaper's personal column and to which he received three replies: from a Lady Severn, a Miss Droplet, a Miss Single. Answering, he made appointments to view. He prepared carefully and practiced speaking with his teeth clenched, which was the best way he had found of hiding his cockneyfied accent.

Miss Single he was to meet in Trafalgar Square, saw the plain creature from a distance and fled. The large Miss

Droplet he also decided against when he went to tea at her flat; apart from being not his type, she had a grip so strong that he feared for his manhood. Lady Severn turned out to be ancient, but, overwhelmed by her title and general splendor, he continued the association and was persuaded to contact and bring along his other two respondents.

Time passed. Sid became involved with Bloomsbury Group Junior, wrote poetry, gave up all hope of orgies, and stopped dreaming of long-haired girls with peasant skirts and dropped drawers. Recently, however, strident nature had reminded him of his original aim in entering the world of art, and, having looked over the available talent, plus knowing full well that the tidal-wave Droplet had for him a desperate passion, he had decided to give Minerva a go.

But now, leaning far forward over the handlebars of his cycle, afraid that if he didn't it might overbalance backward from the monster weight behind, Sid had again changed his mind. That bloody handshake, he thought. Christ. Ruin a man for life. Forget it. Only one thing left. Lower the standards a bit, go for Mrs. Quin. Too old, yes, forty if she's a month, but built. Oooh. Very built.

Sid dwelt with dreamy pleasure on Mrs. Quin's body until action by his passenger brought him back to the scary present. "I'll hold on, if you don't mind," called the Droplet, and her hands slid around him to clasp in his lap. Sid put on screaming speed, sweating with fear.

Undoubtedly Mrs. Jean Quin was built. At forty-two she had the firm body of an eighteen-year-old gymnast growing heavy. Her breasts were as high as the thoughts of men when they looked at her legs, which were as long as the sad female stares drawn by her waist, which was as small as the chances of schoolboys hypnotized by her cavorting hips, which were as well turned as the heads of every age and sex along her route. Mrs. Jean Quin was built.

The summit, when reached, was not, as often happens, a disillusionment. Her conventional prettiness she enhanced by clever cosmetic attention to eyes and lips and year-round use of a sun lamp. Her naturally golden hair, worn in a tail, was a great help. She looked like a model who had retired to the Riviera and taken up eating.

At a delightful rhythmic gait Jean strode down the street and entered the doorway of Lady Severn's apartment house. In the hall she paused on seeing a figure scurry into the darkness beyond the stairs, thinking the scurrier was Virginius Twyce. Deciding she had been wrong, she went on up, her thoughts fondly on the nerve-grotted silver addict. He was a personification of Group character: gentle, vulnerable, hypersensitive, kind, selfless: the true artistic temperament that needed constant help and protection. Which was exactly what she herself could afford all the dear members of the circle, for while she too was an artist, you might say, in a manner of speaking, all things considered, as it were, she had lived out of her shell in the cold world of reality and acquired thereby a useful hardness. She would stand nonsense from no one, especially with respect to her gentle friends.

Jean clenched a fist and felt wistful that there was no one around she could punch in the mouth for insulting her gentle friends.

She rang the bell, was admitted, went around greeting the others.

Lady Severn pecked the new arrival on both cheeks and thought how lucky she had been to have gotten next to Mrs. Quin in that theater queue and discover yet another who was sweet and gifted.

Jem Gate bowed gravely over his handclasp. "Ah," he said, while thinking, with respect, that them was as fine a pair of bosoms as he had ever seen.

Tony Zero kissed Mrs. Quin's hand sulkily, remembering how she had spurned his generosity when he had offered her a special price for that week only of three pounds fifteen.

Jean sat beside her hostess on the couch, feeling pleased with herself for her entrance. She had lost nothing of her art.

Jean Quin was an actress. She was convinced of it. Others

had believed in her as well, applauding her roles in two school plays, her Desdemona with the Methodist Amateurs, her monologues at parties, and the various parts she had played in fund-raising productions for the Mothers' League of Bayswater, in which she had been chosen against great odds (she had never met so many mothers). Yes, she was an actress. She had no qualms about presenting herself as such to the Group or saying that she was "resting," which was equally true; she had been resting for years.

The reason she had never turned professional, despite incessant urgings from a best friend, was that she had a family to raise, two husbands to bury, and a third to divorce. So she had never had the chance to climb to the top. And now that she was familially free, there was no room in the theater for someone of her caliber, able to throw her very soul into a part. Nowadays it was all mumbling and scratching. She wouldn't be in one of their futile plays if they came and begged her.

Jean was not bitter, and acting remained her one true passion. Apart from the theater she was not romantic or a romantic. She had never been in love, though she had always hoped it would happen. Now she had stopped caring. She took no lovers and was unconcerned by the stares and attentions of men. She would rather spend an hour with the Group talking about her past triumphs than an evening with the gayest of blades.

Jean was wondering if Lady Severn had forgotten the story of her two curtain calls so that she could tell it again, as three, when the doorbell rang. She watched the entry of Mr. Fourpenny, the Enfield Valentino, followed by that likable crowd scene, Miss Droplet, who was holding onto the arm of Keystone himself, Virginius Twyce.

Miss Droplet explained, "Found him making faces at the doorbell."

Mr. Twyce shook his head twitchingly, licking at the fleck of blood on his lip. "No, no. I was just about to press it. I've done it before. Pressed many a bell."

"Anyway, we're here, and I can't wait to know what's the emergency."

Jean Quin strode forward. "I think I know."

"Do you, dear?" asked Lady Severn.

"Yes. It must be, it's got to be, the latest outrage by the government."

"Right!"

"In point, the extra shilling of tax announced this morning on all theater seats."

Her face dulling with fondness, the hostess said, "You're so clever, Jean."

"But why the meeting?" asked Sid Fourpenny through his teeth, looking at Mrs. Quin's thighs.

"That will have to wait until dear Miss Single and dear Mr. Cease are here. Who's for tea?"

As the cab swung around a corner, Pat Single saw, standing in wait for a green light, the stocky figure of Relentable Cease. She gagged with alarm and flung herself down sideways on the seat. Had she been seen? The thought made her tremble.

Pat was good at trembling. It was one thing she did exceptionally well. She could start a tremble at her ankles, work it up slowly to her head, and then cut neatly back down to her elbows. Once, given a bad fright by a miniskirt, she had trembled in the region of the groin for more than six minutes.

The cause of her present attack was also fear: the fear of discovery. Miss Single was not all that she pretended to be.

What she pretended to be was poor. Her role consisted of wearing secondhand clothes and living in an attic. Although not largely discomforted by her way of life, it did get her down at times, and then she would buy an expensive outfit (to be discarded later) and move for a few days into a luxury hotel. On the whole, she was rather pleased with herself.

The act had started some two years before, one year after her reaching majority and coming into the attractive sum of money left by the only parent she had ever known: a step-uncle, who had made his fortune out of running a postal school for telegraph operators and had died of apoplexy one evening while reading, it was believed, Henry James. At once Pat found herself in trouble. She was beset by fortune hunters, loan seekers, people with toothy smiles wanting to be her friends. She received so much attention and flattery she was in a constant tremble of delight. It had to stop. She kept dropping things on her toes and scalding herself, poking combs in her eyes, and jabbing toothbrushes to the back of her throat.

It had been lonely in the attic. She had been pleased to find that item in the personal column. In answering, she had only had companionship in mind. She never thought of marriage. The one time she had allowed herself to so think, while walking, she had trembled to such an acute extent that she shuffled herself into the path of an oncoming car.

Even so, she had been relieved when the poet, Mr. Fourpenny, failed to keep the appointment. How could she possibly converse with a real poet? True enough she had written some verses of her own, which had been published in the small magazines, and she had translated into modern Greek the whole of Keats, Shelley, Byron, and Browning, and she had read every line ever widely published in the English language; but these were as nothing compared to the work and knowledge of a *real* poet. What if he started talking about fourteenth-century Japanese verse?

He had not shown up. A few days later, however, he called and with only an oblique, impressive reference, truly esoteric, to Klondike Kate, a poetess of whom in her ignorance she had never heard, took her along to Bloomsbury. Her loneliness was over.

Pat sat up and looked through the cab's rear window. No sign of Mr. Cease. Telling herself that she had not been seen, she calmed. She also told herself that in any case she could have made an excuse—the driver was an old friend who had offered her a free ride. There was no reason to suppose that Mr. Cease, who was nice, they all were, all nice, would go into Lady Severn's announcing that Miss Single was really rich, a user of cabs, and that the Group should shut her out for telling lies. There was no danger of their wanting her for her money and delighting her into the permanent shakes; they were too decent. But if they did find out that she had been lying, they might conclude that she had lied about her creative life, which would undoubtedly be the end.

Pat, in defense against the brilliance of the other members, had sold herself to them as a ceramicist. It was not a complete lie, since she always had been interested in ceramics and was now in the process of learning, having bought a potter's wheel and a small mountain of clay. She had bought as well a gross of bowls and jugs, for window dressing. She felt fairly secure.

Seeing destination close, she stopped the cab and paid, giving a one hundred and ten percent tip. She stood in a doorway. She would wait for Mr. Cease and put her mind completely at rest.

Pat was a plain girl with straight brown hair cut level with the bottoms of her ears and fringed directly above her eyebrows. Like the model in the Before picture of an advertisement for periodic discomfort pills, she had a pained expression. She never wore cosmetics and looked like a nun out of habit. Her body was flat: front view normal, from the side seeming no thicker than a hangered cloak. As with the model in the After picture, she had a smile of unreserved beauty. It appeared rarely, in public, which was just as well, for when it blossomed in the midst of plainness and shoddiness, people thought it an impertinence, were put out, expecting at the most a sordid grin.

Pat poised herself. Mr. Cease had drawn level on the other side of the street.

Relentable Cease might have been Pat's father, or grandfather, insofar as he had an expression of pain, shabby clothes, and a general look of inadequacy. He was stocky and bald. He had pale, unremarkable features which were perhaps lucky in having their expression, because otherwise they might have oozed off into smooth nothingness.

Pat Single ran across. Mr. Cease greeted her without surprise, without any emotion, as was his wont, and inquired in his slow voice after her health. Pat inquired after his opinion of people who rode in cabs. He said he would think it over and write her a letter. Pat was satisfied. They walked on together.

Tea was over. Bloomsbury Group Junior was formally in session. The members arranged themselves around the room. There had been a polite scuffle to get next to Lady Severn on the couch, Miss Droplet winning (". . . young Minerva, destined one day to startle the art world, was asked by the hostess to sit upon her right"). Another scuffle took place between Tony Zero and Sid Fourpenny to place their chairs directly opposite where sat the delectable Mrs. Quin; finally sharing the position, they sat leaning toward each other while contemplating the mysterious, piquant darkness at the top of Mrs. Quin's legs. The others stood or sat where fancy took them.

Lady Severn was saying that the reason for the emergency meeting was to discuss the government's latest crime, an additional one shilling in entertainment tax on all theater seats.

The assembly cast condolent glances at their actress, who performed a funeral with her eyes.

Jem Gate, relieved that the meeting was not concerned with the commercial aspect of his work, but disturbed to find it connected with politics, was moved to speech.

"Something done."

"Exactly," said Lady Severn. "Something has got to be done."

Everyone nodded. Tony Zero also nodded: He had just formed a firm resolve to make Mrs. Quin a special introductory offer of three pounds five.

Virginius Twyce said nervously, "We've got to . . . to . . ."

"Rise to the occasion," put in Minerva Droplet.

Lady Severn gave her a look of approbation, and Minerva

flushed with pleasure ("The first concrete suggestion came from . . .").

Sid Fourpenny had not minded the smell of Tony's hair oil, but he was not happy with now having Tony's head resting on his shoulder. He stood up—Tony giving only a small lurch—and stated through his teeth, "We can't change the government, you know."

"That's very *true,*" said Lady Severn.

Miss Patricia Single thought it about time she made her presence felt, even though what she had to say might be foolish compared to the pronouncements of her friends. She was young enough, however, to be forgiven.

"It seems to me," she said, "that it's not the fault of the whole of Her Majesty's government."

While the possible truth of this was being discussed, Tony Zero went deeper into his daydream of having Mrs. Quin accept his bargain offer and lead him off to her flat. The others, accustomed to his odd poses, made no mental comment on his dangerous lean.

"Certainly we can't blame the Member for Little East Burwood South," said Miss Droplet. "It's the way his hair curls on the back of his neck."

The hostess agreed.

"The Prime Minister collects silver teaspoons," said Mr. Twyce.

"Well, there you are."

Mrs. Quin: "That man who handles Transport or something, he's got the most marvelous eyes."

Miss Single absolved the Ambassador to Russia because of his lapels, Mr. Twyce and Mrs. Cease built a protective wall around a new female MP who liked cats, and Mr. Gate excused the Minister of Housing, who had once remarked that he considered sculpture a form of art.

Tony Zero, now in the flat of Mrs. Quin, was watching her undress. Having removed her shoes, she was slowly unzipping her skirt.

Miss Single stated, "What it boils down to is, the blame falls on the Chancellor of the Exchequer."

Virginius Twyce said worriedly that it seemed patent the Chancellor was bent on destroying all creative forms. This brought a shocked silence. He became more worried. He said, "Of course not."

Lady Severn smiled grimly. "Of course *yes.*"

Again Jem Gate said, "Something done."

"It seems to me," said Miss Single, her flat body concaving like a cobra's head at her impertinence, "that there's a solution to all this."

"Yes?"

"Get the right honorable gentleman out of office."

"Bravo!" cried Lady Severn, clapping her hands.

"I could be wrong, though," Pat whispered, throwing at Mr. Twyce a look of reproach for having led her on.

The look was not accepted. Virginius, having gotten over his recent worry, had found another: the imminent topple of Tony Zero. Reaching out a surreptitious forefinger, he poked Tony erect, then let his belly balloon with relief.

Tony noticed not his change in position. He was deeply engrossed in Mrs. Quin's striptease. She had now taken off her skirt and was rolling down her stockings.

All unaware of the actions of her imagined self, Jean Quin was exchanging with the others glances of satisfaction. "That's that solved," she said with a ladies-in-retirement gesture.

Mr. Cease almost rubbed his hands together. "Didn't take us long to find the answer, did it? No."

Sid Fourpenny: "Nothing to it. *Out of office.*"

Pat Single, to her own annoyance, asked the ridiculous question, "But how?"

Smiles slumped.

Into the gloom Minerva Droplet said brightly, "Let's put it to the vote."

Everyone looked uncomfortable. This could very well be above their heads. Lady Severn mused that it must be frightening at times to be so intelligent.

"Mean," said Jem Gate, made eager by the hint of politics, "vote him out?"

Minerva thought that this was very likely what she had

meant. She nodded wisely, glancing at Mr. Fourpenny to see if he was being attentive ("I was struck by Miss Droplet's keen grasp of current affairs as she led us along . . .).

Virginius Twyce announced, "There's not enough of us."

"Then that's out," said Lady Severn, briskly moving the bridge beyond the tricky current. "What else is there?" She knew what else there was. She wondered how long it would take to get there.

Mr. Fourpenny said, "Have him fired or make him resign."

"Well done," breathed Jean Quin. She was always dazedly pleased whenever one of these artistic souls showed a glimmering of understanding in respect of reality. The only one who never left his ivory tower, she thought, looking at the one, was young Tony, a poor dear of such horrid prettiness that if he were in the theater he would be doomed forever to the chorus.

His eyes were fixed on her own person, but she knew by those eyes' blankness and the tongue tip protruding at the corner of his mouth that the owner of his thoughts was not herself.

Mrs. Quin was, of course, wrong. She would have been disconcerted could she have seen the mental picture of herself, naked from the waist down and turning a slow circle for Tony's inspection.

Flushed with success at having drawn praise from the desirable older woman, Sid Fourpenny went on to amplify his statement.

"What I mean is, we got to either have him fired or make him resign."

Mr. Cease nodded. "I see what you're driving at."

"I mean, you know."

"Yes."

"I suggest," Virginius Twyce said, "if you'll excuse me, that the best way to get him sacked is to bring him into disgrace."

"I second that," said Relentable Cease.

"And the best way," offered Miss Droplet, "is to drag up something loathsome from his past."

Jean Quin winked. "Or invent something."

"But is that fair?" Miss Single blurted. She went into a short bout of trembling, cursing her stupidity, when the actress showed the logic of ethics with, "Is the tax fair?"

"Or," suggested Sid Fourpenny, wanting to be flushed again, "there's the resignation bit. Get him to *resign,* see."

To his disappointment Jean Quin didn't say "Well done" before she said, "A scandal, that's what we need. I can think of some beauties."

"Lynched," said Mr. Cease. "Get the people roused enough so they'll drag him out and lynch him."

Lady Severn: "I like that. I must say, I do like that. It's got something."

"Might take a long time, though," said Virginius Twyce nervously, "getting the masses worked up to fever pitch."

Frowning, Jem Gate said, "Vote him out."

Teeth well clamped, Sid Fourpenny said a grim, "The sack or resignation."

Lady Severn asked if there were any more suggestions. There were not. She said, "I have one myself," adding so that mind-wandering-lonely-as-a-cloud Tony would not be left out of things, "It was suggested to me earlier by our Italian member."

"Yes?" asked the Group, glancing at Tony, who was unaware of the fleet attention. In his mind's cinema Mrs. Quin had removed the clothes from her upper body and was now completely naked as she beckoned him toward her bed.

Lady Severn said, "The suggestion is—assassination."

There followed a long silence. No one knew what to say. And it was best not to laugh, because Lady Severn might not be joking.

Lady Severn was not. "I am glad," she said, "that nobody is actually against the idea. And only think, it would make us a real true organization with ideals and . . . things. We would be striking a blow for freedom, for art, for equality. *You know.*"

There was a good deal of throat clearing. Sid Fourpenny,

feeling a little unreal, asked, "You mean we should kill the Chancellor?"

"Yes, dear."

"Oh."

"Of course, if any of us happen to be opposed . . ." Her circling gaze met only blankness.

Sid: "But what about my sackings and resignings?"

"Oh, we'll give them a try, too. We'll try all three. It will be quite jolly. Now, since none of us is against the plan, let's find out who's for it. We'll begin with me. I say aye. Mrs. Quin?"

Jean, now that the first shock had passed, was rather taken with the idea of an assassination. It was on a grand scale. It smacked of intrigue, trench coats, and Greta Garbo. It was terribly dramatic. It was marvelous theater.

She said, "Aye."

"Mr. Fourpenny?"

Feeling Mrs. Quin's eyes upon him and thinking of his income tax, Sid said gruffly, "Aye."

"Miss Single?"

Pat said a whispered aye because what an established poet could do an aspirer could safely copy, and in any case she could always change her mind later, and furthermore none of them was serious.

"Mr. Cease?"

After four ayes, Relentable would not have dared come out in opposition. He said, "Aye."

"Mr. Twyce?"

Nay would have meant no more Bloomsbury Group Junior. Virginius said, "Aye."

"Mr. Gate?"

Jem saw the appeal in Lady Severn's eyes and gave his aye. But he had already decided. It was not an easy decision, was, indeed, possibly the hardest of his life. He made it, however, and thought grimly that he would stick to it whatever happened.

"Miss Droplet?"

Minerva paused (". . . all eyes were hanging breathlessly on . . .") before voting with the majority for the same reason as Virginius, the reason why most members felt a certain disquietude: It was too late to say nay; nay meant out.

"Mr. Zero?"

In his steamy imagination Tony was limb-locked with Mrs. Jean Quin in the final frenetic throes of the act of love.

"Mr. Zero!"

The call pierced Tony's concentration, pierced it at the worst possible moment. He shot to his feet. Bewildered and frightened like someone slapped from sleep, he walked stiffly to the door and left the flat.

After his footfalls on the stairs had died, the emptiness of surprise was broken by Jem Gate, who spoke for everyone when he said, "Gone."

"Walked out," Mr. Cease murmured.

Lady Severn looked sad. Minerva Droplet patted her hand. "Never mind, love. Let's forget it for now."

Mrs. Quin said, "Yes, let's get down to making plans."

Lady Severn sat in contented solitude by the fire. Her excitement over the future had waned to an enjoyable simmering. She was highly taken with the idea of accomplishment. Bloomsbury Group Junior would be a moving force in the history of art. Their intentions were honorable, their aims of the most noble. It was gorgeous to have at last something to fight for (Madge had felt a terrible loss on the passing of the Lord Chamberlain). It was gorgeous to be doing something in which one believed totally. It was gorgeous to have such staunch friends, who were also true believers. They must be so, for otherwise why should they have fallen in so readily with the destruction of the evil that plagued the nation? There was no possibility of financial gain; therefore, money out, love was in; love of an ideal, love of the victory of reason over injustice. They, like her, looked forward hand in hand to the day when all over the country, in mansion and hovel, people would sink on bended knee and give thanks to that small band of the faithful, those dedicated nine men and women who . . .

Madge Severn spoiled the smoothness of her brow with a melancholy frown. The cause was Tony Zero.

What had made him act that way? she thought. The poor sweet boy. It was sad. But really, he had not created disappointment. There was nothing to fret about in that direction. Nor was there a dread that he would lead the others into non-Group activities. That was impossible. Quite, quite impossible.

Lady Severn shook her head firmly; less firmly; stopped shaking; nodded. Her vivid, artistic imagination could picture the scene. The others came bursting into the room, threw their hats in the air, and announced that they were going to turn political and vote for the reelection of the Chancellor.

Madge shuddered. The picture, however, was wrong, and she found its error and peace of mind. Everything was going to be all right: None of her friends wore hats.

The cafeteria was noisy with clatter as people toughly manhandled crockery from trays to tables to show they didn't care and knew very well they weren't being looked at.

In a dim corner sat three of the conspirators: Miss Droplet, Miss Single, Mr. Cease. They were drinking tea in secret sips and nibbling at buns which were partly hidden in their hands.

Unhappy with the result of the past hour, Pat Single was trying to boost her spirits by continually running through and adding to a list of history's poet-rebels.

Minerva Droplet, holding her mammoth buttocks tight so they would not sag over the rim of her chair, was thinking about Mr. Fourpenny. Since it seemed obvious that he was mad about her, calling at her flat and everything, why had he rushed away from Lady Severn's like that when she had given his shoulder an encouraging squeeze?

Relentable Cease was more excited than he had been in ages, since his first visit to the Bloomsbury flat after meeting

Lady Severn at a public library. He was excited by the immediate past and by the promise of the future. His hand still tingled from the ceremony when, like the others, he had sworn a terrible oath to secrecy on a book by E. Phillips Oppenheim. The future, he thought, now that he had become used to the plan, would bring many a thrill. The question was, what part could he himself play?

Miss Droplet was to write the Chancellor love letters, which, it was hoped, would come to public light. Miss Single had been assigned a special task. Twyce would be in charge of equipment. Mr. Fourpenny had claimed the envied position of production manager and was also to write the Group's slogans. Mr. Gate had said, mysteriously, that he had a plan of his own. Mrs. Quin would employ her theatrical talents to vamp the male staff of Number 11 Downing Street in the hope of discovering the Chancellor's sordid secrets.

"What can you do, dear Mr. Cease," Lady Severn had asked, "that is connected with your art, composing?"

Relentable had mumbled that he might try his hand at creating a signature tune for the Group and meanwhile would go on acting as messenger.

Trouble was, he thought, he was not really, not *really* really, a composer, otherwise he might have been able to come up with something. He had, to be sure, a thoroughly musical background—no less than forty years with the Northern Philharmonic Orchestra, from whom he received a pension—and he often whistled to himself little tunes right out of his own head, but that wasn't exactly being a composer, exactly. He would have to think of something, not only to salve his conscience but to repay Lady Severn for her gift of happiness

"What about that Tony?" Minerva Droplet asked.

Pat said, "He seemed not to be in complete agreement with us."

"I wonder if he'll, you know, talk."

Relentable was startled. "Surely not."

"He didn't take the oath of silence, after all."

Miss Single: "So he's got a perfect right to talk if he wants. Fair's fair."

They debated the rightness of a person talking if he wanted. Pat finally conceded that no one had a right to talk without asking permission first. They agreed that if Tony asked the Group for permission, they would vote for a refusal.

Soon they parted, leaving one at a time for safety and giving in farewell the secret password, which was "hello."

Jean Quin, her coat collar turned up, slunk in and out of doorways, flattened herself against walls, stood under a lamp, languidly smoked several cigarettes, flashed her eyes around until they ached. She was steeping herself in the part of Greta Garbo as Mata Hari.

It would be the greatest role of her career. She only prayed that nothing would happen to cancel the plan.

Jem Gate had been in the West End once already this evening. Unable to find a parking space for his Rolls truck, he had headed back to Bloomsbury. He had parked there and returned in a taxi to Soho.

Now, alighting to pay, it occurred to Jem, his private plan in mind, that here was opportunity golden. In any town on earth, whatever you wanted, a cab driver was the man to ask. He knew where everything was to be found, good, bad, or different. Possibly all he had to do to be whisked off to a sinister den was explain to this man what he had in mind.

Holding the money in his hand, Jem asked, "Killer?"

"Eh?"

"Killer."

"Killer?"

"Yes."

"Killer Street?"

"No."

The cabbie frowned. "Road, Square, Avenue, Mews?"

"No. Killer."

"Killer Theater?"

"Seats," Jem said, thinking of the new tax. "Shilling extra."

"You'll give me a shilling extra for some theater seats?"

"No."

The man gave a faint whine, tried feebly and unsuccessfully to get his fare from Jem's hand and went on a new tack "Are you maybe looking for a man named Killer?"

"*Is* killer."

"You're looking for a man who's a killer?"

"Professional. No amateurs."

Face twitching, the man said dazedly to his steering wheel, "He's looking for a man who's a killer."

"So am I."

Jem was surprised when, without farewell or money, the man took his cab off with a fast leap. Perhaps, Jem thought, he had gone to fetch the required person. But no, Jem wasn't kidding himself it was going to be as easy as that. It might take hours.

He put the money away, musing that some types would do anything for a laugh, and began to stroll in Soho. On the same muse, he gave a dutiful smile.

Jem had come to Soho because it was the most wicked place he knew of. He thought soon, however, as he looked about the narrow yet well-lit streets and at the fine shops that you couldn't believe a thing you read in the papers. There was nothing the slightest bit sinister. But he was pleased at last to notice three boys, playing marbles, who should have been in bed hours ago.

His plan, he told himself, was good. It would solve the whole problem, keep them from getting involved, which could turn out awkward: prisons and so on, expensive lawyers. With a professional killer there would be no worries, no fuss or bother, a nice clean job—one he personally could never do in a million years.

He came into a street narrower and less bright than the others. Midway down he was brought to a stop before a small, scabby bookshop; before, more exactly, that shop's side display case of advertisements and photographs. The pictures were of naked females, each with a note attached to say that the lady was a model and available. The names were all French, the measurements dubious, the addresses Enquire Within.

Dismissing the girls as overdone of breast, Jem read the scribbled or typed ads. Several were promising, offering to go anywhere and do anything legal. Jem cynically refused to be taken in by the "legal"; he entered the shop.

A fat bald man rose from a chair behind the counter. Jem told him, making himself quite clear this time, "Want a killer."

The man laughed pleasantly. "Haven't heard that in years. A killer, eh? A real killer-diller?"

"Yes, please."

"Well, you came to the right place."

"Professional."

"Absolutely," the man said. "What did you have in mind? Blonde, brunette, redhead?"

"No matter."

"What about, shall we say, method? There's a cute little number very good with a whip."

Jem shook his head. He wouldn't want it to be anything too messy.

"Don't fancy a bit of the old fladge, eh? Well, look, you tell me what you've got in mind exactly."

"Gun."

The fat man nodded with an appreciation not entirely void of envy. "That's kinky, that is. Gun, eh?"

"Prefer it."

"Well, there's a girl I can phone for you, real way out, wears . . ."

Jem tutted. "No girls." He somehow could not see a female as a hired assassin. He had his wife and mother to think of.

"*Oh,*" said the man, repeating deep bows to convince of the extent of his understanding. "Now I'm with you, now I see what you mean."

"Killer."

"Certainly, certainly, I know the very boy. A nice young lad training for the diplomatic corps."

Jem shook his head. "No."

"Well, maybe it's the secret service. I can't keep up. There's so much of it about these days."

"Man," said Jem, who was not sending any boys to do the job.

"A man? Not young? I must say"—envy breaking through —"you do have your own ideas on sex."

"Sex?" sizzled Jem. His mind began to grapple with, to prevent from closing in on, a horrible truth, which nevertheless prevailed. Jem was disgusted and outraged. He snapped, "Police!"

The man goggled. "You want a *policeman?*" he gasped in joyous envy-rid admiration. "That's *real* kinky!"

Realizing that he could under the circumstances not complain to the police, Jem turned and stamped out, pausing in the doorway only long enough to be unable to think of a suitable retort.

Above the shop's modern front a writhe of neon spelled out, "FOURPENNY FOR ALL YOUR GREENS." The store knelt sheepishly alone in the center of a long residential street.

With a roar vicious and dramatic Sid brought his motor-assisted bicycle to a halt. He left it curbed and entered the shop, slamming the door. He was annoyed. That bloody dago, he fumed, was nothing but a pain in the arse.

Sid had left the meeting close on the heels of Mrs. Quin and had walked along at her side making pointed remarks about the weather. She was responding well when, reaching the corner, they were leaped at by Tony Zero, who babbled incoherently, gripped Jean Quin's arm, and drew her away. Thwarted in his newfound resolve to be kind to older women, Sid had stumped back to his machine.

Even now, at home, his fury screeched on. He was unable to sit still. He circled the shop, kicking at sacks, swearing with his teeth far apart, laughing harshly. At last he went out to his bicycle and clattered off, flinging his protest into the face of the world by driving in the middle of the road, no lights on

Virginius Twyce sat nervously in his bed-sitter, whose furnishings consisted in the main of a bed and a chair. Between his teeth he gripped a pencil to prevent himself from biting his lips. He was worrying about his first project as head of equipment—the buying of a lock and chain, the cost of which had been borne by popular subscription. The more he thought about the venture, the more improbable it became. He saw himself walking into an ironmonger's and stating his business.

The shopkeeper narrows his eyes. "A lock and chain?"

"Er, yes. If it's all right."

The eyes take in every detail of the sinister stranger, who has been a customer now for several years. "That's a very funny thing to want."

"Well . . ."

"A lock and chain, of all things."

"I know it sounds odd, but—"

"What would you be wanting with a lock and chain?"

"It's—it's for a friend."

The shopkeeper becomes frighteningly obsequious. "Certainly, sir. Will you wait one moment, sir? Excuse me, sir." He goes into a back room. There is the sound of a telephone receiver being lifted.

Virginius rushed from the imagined scene, back to the present. Coughing at the flakes of varnish his chewing had wrought from the pencil, he hurried to an apologetic cupboard in order to calm himself with his collection of Georgian silver: a thimble, a knife, a spoon with a wooden handle.

The restaurant kitchen was a madness of snarling waiters, swearing cooks, hissing pans, and clattering dishes. Stood apart from the chaos, quietly slicing carrots, was the noble figure of Tony Zero.

Tony had given himself the name of Zero because his real

name was unpronounceable outside his native village. Neapolitans made a mess of it, Romans thought it funny, and it caused the English to blush. Therefore he had chosen to use a name simple yet striking when he arrived in Britain to ply his trade as a gigolo, or, to put it in a more seemly way, as he had put it to Miss Gertrude Stein, to have more scope for his designs on women.

The name had been a success, his designing a flop. While what he had heard was true—that Britain's affluent welfare state having made ditchdigging (or even being out of work from ditchdigging) a financially better career than paid bed companion, the ranks of the gigolo had been drastically thinned, making for a great shortage—he had met with little success. He had spent countless afternoons stopping women on streets. He had stood by store entrances, mentioning his availability to likely prospects. He had toured bars and dances, approaching all lone females. Nothing. He got stares, snorts, blankness, and a lot of laughs. He had done very well on the free market, getting picked up by young girls, if he felt in the mood enough to let them, and afterward he had sometimes been able to get money in the shape of a loan. But that was amateur stuff. The Group had also been a failure, so far. Membership stayed static, no new hungry matrons appearing. Regular members were a washout, and making that special offer to Quin after the meeting had come to nought. There was only one thing for it, expensive or not: He would put an announcement in the newspapers and have cards printed.

Tony finished the carrots and stepped outside into an alley to have a smoke. He was not surprised to see, in shadow, a waiting figure, assuming it to be one of the young bits who were always hanging around. He sighed and went across. There was a blur of fast movement, and Tony knew no more, ever. The knife went straight to his heart.

two

Downing Street turns off Whitehall and proceeds for a short, bent way. Traffic has to turn; pedestrians may continue on down a flight of steps into St. James's Park. Those who cannot go down must go back. The street is a dead end.

On either side are houses of undistinguished design and quality, erected by one George Downing, a speculator. Number 10 is the Prime Minister's home, Number 11 the home of the Chancellor of the Exchequer.

This morning, as in most daylight hours, there was a small crowd of sightseers and two or three uniformed policemen. All were concerned with Number 10. Mrs. Jean Quin was concerned with Number 11.

Wearing a raincoat, collar upturned, a man's felt hat, brim downturned, dark spectacles, and the half smile of someone who, used to living dangerously, finds the enemy's proximity merely amusing, Jean Quin stood on a corner of the street at the Whitehall end and kept a cynical eye on the residence of H.M. government's Chancellor of the Exchequer.

Two days had passed since the death of Tony Zero, two days of inactivity owing to the observance of mourning, as decreed by Lady Severn. Everyone had been most upset by Tony's passing. So young, so beautiful, so kind. Were it not for the current involvement in secret, good intentions, the police would have been approached and given every help in tracking down the murderer, who, everyone agreed, must be a jilted girlfriend maddened by jealousy. This being out and attendance at the funeral considered risky, Bloomsbury Group Junior made do with a solemn gathering at Miss Droplet's; Mr. Cease led the singing in "Come Back to Sorrento," and Mr. Fourpenny recited a poem he had written for the occasion, a moving quatrain which caused Miss Single to tremble on account of its perfection (she was particularly taken with the opening line: "There was a dark-eyed, sallow idol from the north of Italee").

There had been a disturbing moment after Lady Severn had mentioned the note in the newspaper report which had informed the Group of Tony's death; the note saying that, as the victim appeared to have no family or friends, he was being buried by the Sons of Italy Club.

"No friends," said Lady Severn. "If they only knew."

Each person had thought the same thing, that he or she was equally as friendless outside the Group, as equally alone and lacking in relations, as equally a social misfit. Each person had then fought off this cruel moment of truth, being terrified lest the other members, who were surely loaded with non-Group friends on account of their brilliance and talent, should in some supranormal way manage to read these horrid, pathetic thoughts. The brief silence had ended in a sudden babble of meaningless talk.

Mourning officially over now, the Group was back on the job.

An hour passed. The scene changed little in Downing Street. Jean continued to dawdle on the corner. Nothing happened except that she was approached by four men who wanted to know either the correct time or where it was they had seen her before or the way to Downing Street. The shrift she gave them was exceeding short.

At close to noon the door of Number 11 swung in. Appeared a man in striped trousers and bowler. About thirty, nasty-sharp face, he strode along the street as if he held its mortgage and cared nothing about money.

Turning the corner opposite Jean's post, he walked away, sideways, an arm signaling at passing taxis. Jean began to follow. She clicked her tongue in Garboish annoyance when a cab slid to a stop beside the man and she saw no other cabs approaching. Her prey was as good as lost, unless—

She made a fast, brave decision. Running forward, she grabbed the taxi door as it was being closed behind him by the passenger. She gasped, "Emergency!"

"Eh!" said the man.

"Now, now," said the driver.

Jean lifted one foot inside, exposing a goodly length of inner thigh. "Please," she said, tremble-voiced. "I need a taxi. It's an emergency."

"I see," said the passenger, head down, peering.

"Now, now," said the cabbie. "First come."

"You needn't give the taxi up. Just let it take me to my place first. I don't live far."

"In that case," said the man, chin on chest.

"I don't ask for the moon," pleaded Jean, refusing to be allowed victory without a fight, "I don't ask for gold, I only ask for your taxi."

"All right," the man mumbled, his contortioned head sinking toward his knees.

"Now," said the cabbie.

Jean gave up and got in. She gasped out her address while settling herself close beside the man from Number 11, whose position and expression had returned to normal. He was, Jean realized, one of those people who cannot help having a façade of nastiness.

After a pause following her thanks, the passenger said drearily, "Nice weather."

"I can't stand emergencies, can you?"

"Marvelous for the time of year. No."

Jean snuggled closer, hip against hip. "I feel I can tell you, Mr. . . ."

"Green-Jones."

"I'm Ninotchka," she said huskily.

"It's a name you don't come across often," he grated, "Green-Jones."

Jean showed the tip of her tongue. "Mmm."

"An old family name, actually."

"As I was saying, Green, I feel I can tell you. There's something—Oh, by the way, what's your occupation?"

"Secretary. Private secretary to the Chancellor of the Exchequer."

Jean gripped his bicep with affectionate pleasure. She had scored a bull's-eye first time. She had been worried that he might have been in Downing Street merely to read the gas meter or collect rent.

"I *knew* there was something about you. A man of power!"

Green-Jones' face twisted with a sadistic smile. "Well, you know, one tries."

"That's why I instinctively felt you'd be a tower of strength. It shows, you see."

"I do, ah, have rather an appointment for lunch."

"How lucky I am," said Jean, stroking the bicep, "actually sitting next to the Chancellor's right-hand man. The power behind the throne."

"It's with an old school friend."

"Yes?" murmured Jean, stroking away.

"Never liked him."

"People from the past can be a nuisance to those who've climbed to dizzying heights."

"Ah, what was this emergency of yours, miss?"

For the rest of the journey Jean, gently muscle stroking, performed her Little Girl Lost role to the gilt and plush of Green-Jones' manner, explaining that she was sure she had left the bathroom window open, and one read in the papers of so many burglaries.

The cab stopped. "What *would* I do," huskied Jean, "if I found a burglar? Me, a woman alone, helpless, vulnerable."

"The thing is, I believe, one has to be quite firm with these people."

"Helpless, vulnerable, alone in my cozy flat with its central heating and large double bed."

"Stand no nonsense."

"Inner spring mattress."

"Ah, if I might make a suggestion."

With Jean's shy agreement Green-Jones paid off the cab and accompanied her up to her flat. There was no burglar, and the bathroom window, three inches square, was firmly closed. Jean insisted against no resistance that her guest accept a rewarding drink. She settled him on the couch with a gin and excused herself, swayed into her bedroom, and stripped naked. There was no time for a subtle, drawn-out campaign.

Wearing a robe, she went back to the living room doorway and languished there. She asked if it met with her guest's approval. Green-Jones said that he rather preferred Gordon's. But his hand was unsteady as it raised the glass.

"Oh, Green," breathed Jean, her brow sorrowing, "I must confess to you that I lied. I knew the window was closed. The fact is, I had to meet you, get to know you. When I saw you striding along Whitehall, something moved inside me. I felt a burst of heat."

"I say."

"It was love, Green," Jean went on, feeling emotional, acting what she had hoped for and never found. "Love at first sight. Love of the finest, most honorable kind. I knew at that moment that I would follow you to the ends of the earth."

"Good show."

"I'm yours, Green. All yours." She opened the robe and let it fall from her shoulders.

Putting down his drink, Green-Jones began to untie a shoelace. He said with a mild snarl, "Thanks awfully."

The hardware store was large and busy, which was the reason it had been chosen, there being safety in the anonymity cloaked upon one by a shop of such attributes. Or so had reasoned Virginius Twyce.

He stood, Virginius, spectacles partly steamed from the heat of his agitated body, peering at the shop from around a lamppost. He peered and knew at once, deep in his heart, that he could not go through with the assignment. It was too dangerous, he hadn't the nerve, he was sure to make a slip, give the game away, plunge the whole secret project into public chaos. His stomach cringed at the thought of the ruin he could bring down on his friends.

Clinging weakly to the lamppost Virginius worried his mind for a solution. One came with gratifying ease when his roving, agonized gaze fell on an approaching schoolgirl. He gave a light whinny of hysterical relief.

The girl drawing level, Virginius leaned around the post and said, "Yoo-hoo," followed by, "Ha-ha."

She stopped. "Yer what, mate?"

"Would you like to earn sixpence, run a tiny weeny little errand for me?"

The girl came closer. "Run a what?"

Virginius realized immediately his mistake. The child was obviously a cynic; her nostrils gave her away. She would grasp with speed the sinister implications of his request. Pretending to play along, she would fly instead to the nearest police station and gabble, "Listen, listen, there's a man wants me to buy a lock and chain!"

"Go away," snapped Virginius.

The girl stepped even closer, showing interest. "You all right, luv?"

"Shoo," Virginius said, retreating behind the post.

"I've got me first-aid badge."

"*Leave.*"

"I'm very good with shock and broken arms."

Virginius noticed with horror that nearby a woman was watching, one eye closed in malicious concentration. It was patent that she was the type who made a career out of unmasking child molesters.

He stood back from the post. "Many thanks," he jerked in a loud, carrying voice, grinning at the girl. "I am sure I shall find the place to which you have directed me. I am expected there to meet my children. Yes, I have children of my own, all girls, all your age. Good day."

He strode off, ankles jellified, glasses dripping.

Fifteen minutes later the assignment was completed, and Virginius sat, a mammoth of calm, in a taxi headed for the West End.

A telephone kiosk had given him the idea. His handkerchief over the mouthpiece, he called the ironmonger and placed his order, which he asked to be brought outside when he came to collect in a cab, he being too sick to walk. It had worked like a lucky charm for the congenitally lucky.

Cuddling his parcel, Virginius smiled at the thought of how cleverly he had circumvented the girl's rotten intentions and hoodwinked the molester addict.

In Leicester Square he left his cab and went down to the underground. At the appointed spot, in an escalator-sided cavern, Mr. Cease stood waiting.

Virginius said, "Hello."

"Hello."

"What's the password?"

"Hello."

"Hello. What's the password?"

"*Hello.*"

"Hello. Give me the password."

Mr. Cease frowned, almost. "What *is* the matter with you?"

"No, it's not."

"I'm sorry?"

"It's not that, either."

Mr. Cease tutted. "Virginius, what are you on about?"

"The password. You've got to give it."

"I have. Several times. Hello."

"Hello, Relentable. Have you forgotten the password?"

Mr. Cease gave in. He had a headache. "Yes."

"So have I. I was hoping to bluff though, get it from you first."

"I see."

"I'd know it if I heard it."

"Why don't you just give me the parcel?"

Virginius looked doubtful. "I dunno. You could be anyone."

"So could you, for that matter."

"You're right, by heaven."

"You could be trying to give me something worthless."

"I think we're in trouble."

Saying that he had suddenly remembered, Relentable explained that the password was "hello." Virginius said of course it was.

"All I needed was to hear it, you see."

"Yes. Ready now? Hello."

"Hello."

The package changed hands. After a short chat, the men parted with a final hello. Virginius went off to get a sandwich before returning to work, where, he told himself worriedly, he would have to make a point of not mentioning anything about locks or chains.

Mr. Green-Jones, private secretary to the Chancellor of the Exchequer, lay in blissful repose with his head between the breasts of his mysterious new mistress. He felt a gorgeous abandonment, which feeling, he craftily mused, storing the fact for future use, could be increased if he took off more than just his shoes.

Ninotchka sighed. "Happy, Green?"

"In the extreme," he murmured nastily.

"What would the Chancellor say if he could see you now?"

"By George!"

"Really?"

Green-Jones mumbled, musing on the strangeness of this exotic creature. He was not surprised when, after answering truthfully her question about his employer, saying he was a fine fellow, she growled like a small dog. Nor was he affected, so different was she, when another answer, to the effect that the Chancellor's private life was to him a closed book, brought from her a long, exotic groan. But surprised he was when, after adding that he had been working at Number 11 less than a week, she pushed him onto the floor and jumped on his stomach.

"Oh, my darling, my own true special love, if only you were here now, sitting on my knee . . ."

Minerva Droplet paused in her writing. That sounded not quite right, she thought. Besides, it was somewhat forward. This was only the third love letter to the Chancellor. Best not to rush things. And she had all the time in the world to work at composition. ("Miss Droplet, famous now, had at one time been forced to slave in a department store, which job she instantly renounced when she had persuaded the rest of the Group that they should assassinate the Scourge of Britain.")

Minerva crossed out the last phrase. As she sat pondering the next, from below came a sound signaling a post delivery. Stepping out onto the landing, she shouted down to ask if there was anything for her and heard faintly through the reverberations of her cry a frightened voice answering yes. She thudded downstairs.

There was one letter. It came from Downing Street. Minerva knew with a thrill that it must be a reply to the first of her love letters, which she had posted two nights before. Slitting the envelope, she was assailed by doubt: Had she done right in giving her name and address?

All emotion drained when she pulled out the enclosure: a printed form with a line through the latter part of Sir/Madam; it thanked her for her contribution to the Anti-entertainment Fund.

Minerva stumped upstairs. Obviously she had been too restrained. What was needed was some real passion, burning kisses, crushing embraces, the lot.

Discarding her half letter she began again. "My darling demon lover, my own erotic love, my sizzling sexy Sid—"

"Eh?" said Minerva. Angrily blushing, she flung the page aside and made a fresh start.

Downing Street. None of the official or touristic loiterers

took any notice of the tall woman who entered and strode to the end, for there was nothing too remarkable about wearing a tweed suit with a black hat fronted by a half veil. Nor did anyone give a second glance to the plain girl who followed a minute later, despite the fact that she came close to disappearing when she passed side-on. A third arrival did draw the attention of two constables; but only briefly; being English, they quickly averted their gaze, not wishing to embarrass the man by staring at the mysterious lump under his coat.

Lady Severn, Pat Single, and Relentable Cease grouped at the street end. Lady Severn said, "So far so good."

She smiled. It was her first smile since the murder of Tony Zero. His death had upset her greatly. She mourned for the passing of a friend and for a loss the world of design would never know about. With sadness and avidity she followed the press reports of the investigation, which was centered on tracing the murder weapon, as alibis had been provided by all Tony Zero's known girlfriends—six waitresses, three shopgirls, nine students, and a demonstrator from a family-planning clinic.

There had been no connection discovered between Tony and Bloomsbury Group Junior, whose existence, indeed, was known only to its members. Any one of them, Lady Severn thought with satisfaction, could be murdered without his connection with the Group coming to light. It was nice to know, comforting.

Pat Single did not answer Lady Severn's smile. Even had she wanted to, she would have been unable to; she was having trouble enough keeping her head still, her neck was trembling so. She did not like this situation at all.

Mr. Cease did answer Lady Severn's smile. Publicity, pictures in the paper, it all sounded exciting and unlonely.

"There's the signal," Madge Severn said, nodding toward Whitehall, where Sid Fourpenny stood waving a handkerchief over his head. "Things are moving along at a nice brisk pace."

"I hope," said Relentable, "that he made a proper job of telephoning the newspapers."

"I don't feel terribly well," murmured Miss Single.

"Stage fright, my dear." Lady Severn raised both arms high above in a victory clasp, at which Sid Fourpenny pocketed his handkerchief and strolled off.

"It's my stomach," whimpered Pat, clasping her neck.

"Forward!" called Lady Severn. She led the way to the railings of Number 11, where she halted smartly. "Positions, tools!"

While Pat Single, slack with reluctance, stood herself with her back to the railings, Relentable Cease brought out and unwrapped his package, unwrapping the lock and chain.

Madge Severn looked around. The nearby crowd was watching with lip-licking fierce-eyed intentness the delivery of a laundry basket at Number 10.

"Proceed," Madge said.

Relentable stepped to Miss Single, who flattened herself against the rails, head back, and glared fearfully at the sky. She felt the chain circle her neck, heard it clank around a paling and heard the lock click. She was held tight.

Mr. Cease put the key in his pocket.

Lady Severn asked, "Shouldn't one swallow it or something?"

Before he could answer, a policeman had appeared at their side. Middle-aged, face centered by a drooping mustache, he elbowed forward an arm which held three stripes and said sternly, "Can't do that. Against the law."

"I beg your pardon?" said Lady Severn.

"Illegal," the sergeant said, apologetic now, having heard the accents of the Establishment. He nudged his stripes downward in the direction of the discarded wrapping paper. "Litter Act of 1965, contravention of."

"Ah."

"If you don't mind my saying so."

"Not at all."

"Can't do it, you know."

"By the way, I'm Lady Severn."

"Silly, some of these laws," the policeman said, swooping down on the paper and crumpling it out of sight under his tunic.

"Especially the tax laws."

"Rotten they are, m'lady, putrid." He turned crouchingly to Mr. Cease. "It'll be quite all right, your lordship, if you should feel like dropping another slip of paper."

"That's very civil of you," said Relentable absently, glancing over at the crowd.

The people were tensely on their toes or bulging tight tongues beyond their teeth or holding clawed hands suspended in midair: the laundryman, the large basket in his straining arms, was teetering for balance on the curb.

Lady Severn decided enough time had been wasted. "Observe," she told the sergeant, pointing at the stiff, stricken Miss Single. "This girl has a chain about her neck."

"If it's not one thing it's another, m'lady. Style's a funny thing."

"The chain is also around the railings."

"My daughter," confided the sergeant, "married now, thank God, came home one day with her hair dyed white. White!"

"I wonder it didn't turn *you* white," quipped Madge. She and the policeman laughed merrily.

Pat Single gave a tiny moan, the best she could manage with the stricture on her throat. She had just realized something horrible. With her knees growing weaker in their efforts to control the trembling of her thighs, she would soon begin to sink toward the pavement. The chain, tight now, would be tightened even more. She would strangle to death. "Help," she whispered.

"I knew a girl once," said Lady Severn, "who wore her hair brushed down in front of her face."

"How did she see where she was going?"

"She had one of those blind dogs, you know."

"The blind leading the blind, eh?" joked the sergeant. He and Lady Severn shared another jolly laugh.

"Help," outsipped Miss Single.

Mr. Cease thought that the plan was getting nowhere. By now the Chancellor should have been outside, struggling with Pat before a booing crowd and being photographed in doing so by the press. If reporters showed up before the action started, the whole venture would come to nothing.

Relentable interrupted the sergeant, who, wiping his eyes, was talking of a dog he once knew with three legs, and reminded Lady Severn of the business at hand.

The policeman snapped to sad gravity. "I'll be off then. You've got things to do." He backed away. "Does you good though, a decent old laugh."

Mr. Cease said, "This girl is chained to the railings."

"Yes, m'lord." The policeman saluted and marched off.

"Help," seeped Miss Single, fighting against her sagging legs.

"Mr. Cease," Lady Severn said, "do something to attract attention."

Relentable squared his shoulders, strode to a point beyond the crowd, and shouted, "Good heavens! A girl over there is chained to the railings!"

More than one person took his anxious eyes off the laundryman's struggle, looked at Mr. Cease, and then glanced toward the pair at Number 11, whereupon Lady Severn, nodding happy encouragement, made little gestures toward Miss Single, showing her off. The lookers went into reverse, giving Relentable a stare of dislike on their way back to the laundryman, who was now down on one knee.

Mr. Cease returned to Madge Severn. "Perhaps if we waited till that man's finished."

"No time. The gentlemen of the press will be here at any moment."

"What shall we do?"

"Any suggestions, Patricia?"

"Help."

"What did she say?"

"She didn't speak. She's just rolling her eyes around."

"I must say, Patricia, you're awfully good at this sort of thing."

"I agree," Relentable said. "But what shall we do?"

"About what?"

"About getting the Chancellor to come out and get violent with Pat."

"Let's think."

Pat's knees were knocked, her sweat-lubricated hands sinking down the palings. She tried to remember the words of "Nearer, My God, to Thee."

"The direct approach," stated Lady Severn. "Leave it to me. Patricia, prepare to be attacked." She strode to the door and knocked.

The wood swung in. A man who looked like a stage butler said, "No."

"No what?"

"You can't see the C of E."

"I do not wish to see him, my good man. I wish him to be appraised of a highly important matter."

"Which is?"

Stepping back, Madge held out an arm. "Witness. A young lady is chained to the railings."

"Dear me," the butler said, peering out. "How did that happen?"

"It did not happen. She did it herself. She did it intentionally."

"Whatever for?"

"It's a protest. An act of defiance."

The man smiled. "I get you. I understand."

"Thanks. Will you inform the Chancellor?"

"Oh, no. He's having his tea. And anyway, there's no point. You're too late."

"What on earth do you mean?"

"Well, look, it's been done."

"Done?"

"Long ago. You're too late. You've got it."

"Got it?"

"The *vote,*" said the butler. "Votes for women. Pankhurst and that. King's horses."

"I do not know," Lady Severn said, "what you are talking about."

"We *gave* it you."

"Many thanks."

The man smiled thinly. "That's what's wrong with this country today. Women voters."

"I don't do it myself. I'm opposed to it on principle."

The man looked hurt. "You'd vote for me though, wouldn't you?"

"You?"

"I mean, ahm, the Chancellor."

"Of the Exchequer?"

"Yes."

"No. He's a vile beast."

"Watch it, kid," the man rasped. "Remember where you are."

A female voice called from the interior, "Ron, your tea's goin' cold."

"Buzz off," the man said, beginning to close the door.

"Will you tell the Chancellor?"

"As a matter of fact, he just left via his secret underground passage for a fact-finding tour of the East." The door closed.

Lady Severn went back to Mr. Cease. "Nice chap that. He was quite taken with me. Called me kid. He was kind enough to tell me that the Chancellor's not home."

"Shall we wait?"

"Help," tinkled Pat.

"I don't know. He might be ages. He's gone to the East End."

After the interruption of a small, warm cheer from the crowd as the laundryman tumbled his load into Number 10, Mr. Cease said, "We could go and have a cup of tea."

"Yes, and bring one back for Patricia."

Pat Single made a great effort. She strengthened straight

her legs and pushed up with her sweaty hands and gasped loudly, "Take this chain off my neck!"

Lady Severn looked at her thoughtfully. "Perhaps you're right, dear. You always are rather sensible. He might be away till late tonight. Relentable?"

Mr. Cease took off the chain. Pat sank weakly, dizzily, thankfully to the pavement. She found enough strength to shake her head when Lady Severn told her to get up, they were leaving.

Glancing at the crowd, which, now that the laundryman had gone, was shuffling its feet and staring morbidly at the smoke from the chimney of Number 10, Lady Severn said, "Upsy-daisy, dear. Time to go."

"'Sausted," sobbed Pat.

Part of the crowd looked across with interest.

"Please, Patricia. You're making a scene."

"Don't care."

"People are *looking*."

"Let 'em."

"Mr. Cease!" commanded Lady Severn. They took an arm each, raised the floppy girl to a vaguely erect stance, and keeping a tight grip, began to walk up the street, Pat lolling and sobbing and grinning.

Several people shook their heads.

Lady Severn told Pat that her act had been marvelous, that they must be sure to tell Mrs. Quin, that she could safely stop it now, that some other time when the Chancellor was home they would let her do it again, and that come now there was no need to take on so, they knew she was grateful, there was no need for tears.

Gaining Whitehall, Lady Severn said, "How well we did, not getting the Chancellor out to cut up violently. Without the press there it would have been a waste of time."

"Victory is ours," said Mr. Cease damply.

Sid climbed the stairs in Mrs. Quin's block of flats. Now that Tony Zero was out of the way, Sid felt there was no obstacle between himself and Jean Quin. Indeed, being an older woman, she no doubt would be overjoyed at the prospect of having a virile young lover, would jump at the chance, would give herself with enthusiasm, would offer tearful thanks, would treat her young and virile master like a potentate, would indulge in . . .

By the time Sid Fourpenny reached Mrs. Quin's flat he had convinced himself. He was fixed. His point in joining the Group had at last been made.

He rang the bell urgently, and when the door opened, revealing Jean either half undressed or half dressed, he blurted, "Here I am."

"Bully for you," Jean said. She yawned, still dozy from her nap. After feeling sorry for her attack on Green-Jones, she had massaged his bruised stomach. One thing had led to two others. Finally getting him out, she had fallen into an exhausted sleep. Now she felt fine, mellow, and pleased with herself for drawing the most out of a poor subject: Green-Jones had given her all he was able—names and descriptions of the staff at Number 11.

"You knew I was coming, didn't you?" Sid asked with abandon, forgetting his teeth.

"Well, I thought you might. You or Mr. Cease."

"He's too old."

"For all these stairs? Perhaps."

"Stairs," Sid repeated dully, biting. "Er, I came—"

"To tell me about Downing Street. How did it go?"

"Oh." Sid momentarily lost his passion on being reminded of his failure with the newspapers. He had given the handkerchief signal to the team in Downing Street because they were so keen to act and he hadn't the heart to tell them that every paper contacted had said they were giving no more free publicity to the Chancellor, who surely could come up with something more original.

"It was a flop," he said.

"Oh, well."

"Anyway, Mrs. Quin—Jean—what about you? You know, sex."

"I *have* found out a little bit."

Sid winked. "I'll bet you have. Married three times. Well, here I am."

"Good. And I do think you'll be better at it than Virginius Twyce."

"Absolutely," said Sid, loosening his tie.

"Her name's Molly, and she's been with him for years. She's the cook. She should know all about him."

"Who cares about Twyce? Let's go inside, Jean."

"Sorry, dear, no time for socializing, got to go and pick up the next victim. Ta-ta."

The door closed in Sid's gnashing face. He slowly took in what had been said and sorted out what it meant. He slipped back the knot of his tie, tighter and tighter.

Darkness had settled down for the night when Jem Gate parked his Rolls truck in an East End dockland road. He was trying a new area, having become thoroughly disillusioned with Soho. Two nights before, he had asked around for hours, getting nowhere. Soho was vastly overrated.

Not, Jem thought as he alighted, that this looked too promising.

The road, wide and achingly straight, was lined with business places of a glumness that spoke not of opulent sin but cruddy misdemeanor, that did not reek of evil but had a pong of bathroom naughtiness. There were few people about, and these keeping well back from the curbs in their scurry, as if fearful of the boorish traffic, an endless splurge fighting hysterically to leave the city it had earlier fought hysterically to reach.

Dickens, mused Jem, was a bit out-of-date. Still, it was early yet. As the evening drew on, there might very well be strange noises, screams, a woman's voice pleading for mercy, cackles of haggish laughter, slinking figures, snatches of drunken song, loitering toughs, sounds of rapid footfalls, choked cries. Yes, there might very well be. People were now most likely having supper, getting ready for the laughing and slinking and stuff.

Jem began to walk. He walked for half an hour. He saw

nothing more untoward than an Italian restaurant lighted by candles instead of electricity.

Which recalled to his mind the late member of the Group, Tony Zero. It was too bad, he thought. He would miss old Tony. It was funny how things turned out. Alive and dreaming one day, dead the next. But it was the same in everything. The same in politics. You could be right at the top of the heap and then comes an election—

Jem chopped himself off. He refused to think about politics behind Lady Severn's back.

Soon he came to an old-clothes shop that was suitably murky. He went in. He was delighted to find, sitting on a stool and surrounded by rags, an old woman who was definitely of the crone type. He felt sure that if he happened to say the right thing, she would cackle.

Taking a good breath he asked, "Where find killer?"

The crone looked at him with eyes that were, he was pleased to note, beady. "Buy your suit if you like."

"Looking for killer."

"He's not 'ere, Charlie."

Jem stopped himself in time from correcting her on the name. "Know one then?"

"I know Killer Watson, if that's who you're on about."

Jem blinked keenly. "Professional?"

"Does nothink else."

"Any good?"

"He did my son-in-law a foo years back," the crone said, ripping a piece of cloth in two. "I've got no complaints."

"Cheap?"

"It's the way you look at it. Depends 'ow badly you wants someone done."

"Bad enough."

"Well, Killer's the boy. He gives good service. Money-back basis, of course."

"Naturally."

"That's a decent bit of cloth in that suit of yours, Stan."

"Killer Watson?"

The crone sighed. "You'll find 'im in the billiard 'all. A

mile along on the other side. Boy in a green cap—one of mine."

"Thanks."

"Tell 'im as Old Sal sent you," the crone said, brightening, "and I'll get me commission."

"Oh, Mr. Percival," breathed Jean Quin, her brow sorrowing. "I must confess to you that I lied. I knew the window was closed. The fact is, I had to meet you, get to know you. When I saw you striding along Whitehall, something moved inside me. I felt a burst of heat."

"Nothing serious, I trust."

Mr. Percival was short and fat and young. Jean had arrived at Downing Street just as he was leaving and, knowing him from Green-Jones' description to be the secretary to the second secretary, had wasted no time in picking him up.

"It was love," she went on, swaying inside her negligee. "Love at first sight. I knew that you were more than a mere secretary and that I would follow you to the ends of the earth."

"Actually," said Mr. Percival, "you're quite right. I am more than a secretary. Actually, I'm a biographer. I'm writing the C of E's definitive biography."

Jean smiled. "You know all about the Chancellor's life?"

"All, Miss Ninotchka. I possess every one of his little secrets, actually."

With unfeigned eagerness Jean opened the negligee and let it fall from her shoulders. "I'm yours, Mr. Percival. All yours."

The billiard hall was an attic with foul air, desperate lighting, and three gray-green tables. Still breathless from his traumatic dash through the traffic, Jem Gate stood in the doorway and looked around.

No one was playing. Three youths lounged against a wall, showing pleasure in their surroundings by appearing sullen. A pensioner was asleep in a chair. A man in bus-conductor uniform was lazily rolling balls across a green. There were posters advertising VD.

On a bench sat a man of about forty, wearing an emerald-green cap. He was massive without being flashy. He had a round, babyish face and no nose, merely an undercurling ripple an inch above his mouth. With an expression of anxiety he was reading a comic book.

Jem went over to the bench, sat, and asked, "Killer Watson?"

Eyes on the comic, the man said, "I was 'ome last night between the hours of nine and nine thirty."

"Old Sal."

"Old Sal what?"

"Sent me."

The flat face turned. "Oh, ah. I see now as you're not a copper. Yes, mate, I'm Killer."

"Want a job?"

Killer Watson put aside his comic. "Employment's always welcome, sir. Who d'you want done?"

"A friend," Jem said, playing it cautious.

"Them's the best kind."

"Yes?"

"Sure. Know their 'abits, see."

"I see."

"What's he been up to—your old lady's whatsit?" Killer slapped his knee and rumbled out a laugh. "That's a joke. Did you get it?"

"Yes."

"I use it regular. Puts people at their ease, see."

"To business."

"Right. When d'you want 'im done?"

"At once. Tomorrow."

"Yes, I think I can fit you in. And 'ow well, like?"

"*Very* well."

"I mean, 'ow long d'you want 'im out of circulation?"

Jem frowned. "Eternally, course."

" 'Ternally," echoed Killer Watson. "Don't that mean for always?"

"Yes."

"Naw," said Killer, shaking his head and rocking his body. He looked embarrassed. "Naw, mate. I don't go for that permanent stuff."

"Never?"

"Never. Not me. Do 'em, yes. Do 'em *in*, no."

"Why not?"

"You gets nine year if you're caught, see. It's too much. One year I can do, even three. I can eat me porridge with the best of 'em. But them old nines." He shook his head, sucked in air juicily, and rocked.

"Pay well."

"No, mate. Why not let me do you a GBH?"

"Who?"

"GBH. You know, Grievious Bodily 'Arm. That's my line."

"Not enough."

"I'm known for it. I make a right mess of 'em."

"Sorry."

"Look, I'll put you in for a tenner. Ten pounds. It's me slack period."

"Fifty. Permanent."

Killer rocked, looking embarrassed, worried and tempted. "Fifty quid, eh?"

"Cash."

The rocking increased. "Naaaw. 'Ardly worth it—nine year."

"*If* caught."

"It's a fifty-fifty chance. Anyway, it's not my line. Who you want is Portuguese Ned."

"From Portugal?"

"From Stepney. Ned's got a very good name in the trade. You can always find 'im at the Good Samaritan. Likes 'is booze does Ned."

"Losing business."

"I dare say I am. But that's your fault. You won't let me do you a GBH."

"Permanent," Jem said. "Sixty pounds."

"Sixty quid," murmured Killer Watson, licking his lips and rocking gently. "Nine year."

"Soon passes," Jem persuaded, his voice soothing. "Time flies."

Killer's rocking suddenly took on the violence of release. "Naaaaaaw."

Virginius Twyce, sitting on the chair and with his feet propped on the bed, toyed with his silver thimble and his wooden-handled spoon and wondered why the collection was not giving him the pleasure it usually gave. He felt quite odd this evening, and there was no reason why he should. The day had gone well. The purchase had been accomplished cleverly, the transfer safely made, while at the office he had not mentioned locks and chains more than twice. But who knew what the morrow might bring? There would be many dangers before the Group's mission was brought to fruition.

Thinking of dangers, Virginius began to fumble nervously with the silver and drew his bottom lip into his mouth to give it a good chew. He no longer felt odd.

"How was that for you?" asked Jean Quin, asking in earnest, speaking from the terrace of her femininity.

Mr. Percival mumbled an appropriate reply. The sound of his voice reminded Jean that she hardly knew the man, returned her to stern reality. Stroking his hair, she asked him to continue his story of the Chancellor's life.

Mr. Percival rolled over onto his back. "Ah, yes. Where was I?"

"His third birthday."

"Well, the cake was from Fortnum's, and he was given a wooden train which he could pull along by means of a length of string." He paused. "Actually, it was cord. Three-ply."

"Was he a good boy?"

"No," Mr. Percival emphatically said. "It will not have to come out in the book, of course. One is not going to tell the whole truth until after the C of E's time."

"But you're going to tell it to me, aren't you? You do it so well. I am utterly fascinated."

"Yes, thank you, I do believe I have the knack. I get the insights, that's what it is."

"And the Chancellor?"

"Well, Ninotchka, you won't believe this, but ten minutes after being handed that train—it was red, by the way, red with a green cabin, and on the side it said Choochoo."

"Utterly fascinating."

"No more than ten minutes after being given that train, that little boy had broken off one of the wheels!"

"Good God."

Lady Severn, wearing purple silk pyjamas, reached from her chair to the radio and switched off the late-night news bulletin. She felt piqued not to have heard that the Chancellor of the Exchequer had died of a heart attack. Her dislike of the man increased.

Sipping her cocoa she mused that as the National Disgrace angle was getting nowhere and nothing had developed yet toward Chancellor Resigns, it was time to consider Angered Mob Marches on Number 11. The populace was angry enough already, to be sure; all it needed was a little stirring. The thing was, where to start?

Madge had found the answer by the time her cocoa was finished. While she made a note to call the equipment supervisor first thing, she let her mind show pictures, in jerky black and white, of mobs on the march, torches blazing, coils of rope held pointedly in view.

And if that failed, she thought cheerfully, there was always the last resort: Chancellor Assassinated.

The living quarters of the shop named Fourpenny for All Your Greens were silent and dark; dark except for a faint glimmer in the bedroom; a glimmer seeping out from the mound on the bed. Sid, under the blankets, continuing a habit formed in youth, was reading a dirty book by flashlight.

After a time he lay the book aside. He had reached a state which he himself referred to as proper chronic. He turned his mind to matters not of the venereal. Or almost not.

Mrs. Jean Quin. It was obvious she had a thing for him. At her door there, she'd been on the verge of dragging him inside when something had given her seconds. She had remembered something. What she'd remembered could very well be that she had been warned off. And who'd do that? Why, none other than the Droplet, who had a big passion going for him that she couldn't control. She was getting to be a nuisance was Miss Droplet. In fact, something would have to be done about Miss Droplet.

Sid nodded and went back to the venereal.

Mr. Percival, naked, sat propped up with pillows. He was holding a cigarette and a drink. He looked blissfully happy. He was talking.

Jean Quin was listening. She had been listening for hours. She was close to the breaking point. Sitting at the end of the bed, wearing her negligee, she stared at the talker with haggard eyes and decided to risk hurting his feelings, risk ending the promising association.

She leaped in with, "Do you know it's two o'clock in the morning?"

Mr. Percival put an instant stop to his look of bliss. "Am I boring you?"

"Oh, no," Jean weakly insisted. "I'm fascinated."

"I can't say, Ninotchka, that you looked terribly fascinated awhile back when I was describing the contents of his schoolbag."

"I was concentrating on storing them in my memory." Mr. Percival smiled again. "It *is* interesting, actually."

"I've been thinking, though, couldn't we jump ahead a few years?"

"You said you wanted to hear it all."

"I do, I do, but . . . just a few years . . . darling."

Mr. Percival lowered his eyes coyly. "If you'll come here first."

Jean whimpered. The mission, she reminded herself, the sacred mission. She slipped out of her negligee and crawled painfully up the bed.

Ten minutes later, back in her place and robe, Jean prompted with a feeble, "The jump?"

Mr. Percival lit a cigarette. "Very well, I'll tell you what, we'll go way ahead in the story and see our subject when he has attained the age of seven."

Jean coughed. "Thanks."

"He was an excellent student at his new school, Miss Miniker's. His thirty fellow classmates were named as follows: Aiken, Blunder—"

"Er," Jean said, her voice cracking, "didn't he do anything *wrong?*"

"Actually, yes," said Mr. Percival. He cleared his throat. "Rather sticky, this. Lucky it hasn't got about. It came from mixing with bad company, I dare say."

"What . . . did . . . he . . . do?" grated Jean, holding on.

"Broke into an orchard, he and some friends, climbed a wall three feet high. *They stole some apples.*"

"The beast!" Jean sobbed, breaking off the delicate point of her composure. She threw herself facedown. "The swine!"

At four in the morning, Miss Single, who practiced insomnia, was sitting glare-eyed on the floor beside a chair which held a pile of ceramic salad bowls. Pat was unhappy, causing sleep to be more evasive than usual tonight. It wasn't simply that her neck still hurt or that she had not yet recovered her emotional balance from the ordeal in Downing Street; it was the whole situation that made her mind keep ticking. She was unhappy about Bloomsbury Group Junior. Yes, she would admit it. She would repeat it. She was unhappy about Bloomsbury Group Junior.

Cheered an inkling by her moral bravery, Pat got up and went to the corner kitchenette, where she prepared her third cup of tea since retiring. The brew mashed, she poured a cup, took it over to the bed, and began to consider her predicament. She reasoned thus:

She was a simple girl. She had no right to be associating with brilliant people. She should not be getting herself involved with things she did not understand, actions that to her seemed somehow wrong, which showed her want of knowledge and intelligence. Today she should have felt ennobled, uplifted by her experience; she had not; she lacked the necessary superior qualities. She had to stop fooling these fine people by pretending to be on their level. She had to get out of the Group.

Pat gave a gasp of relief. So far so good. The next step was: how?

Hardly had she posed the question before she saw it was not required. She had had the solution all along. All she need do was disappear. Simply stop seeing the Group and move house, leaving no other address. When settled away, somewhere luxurious and quiet, she would write to Lady Severn, making an excuse composed mainly of the truth and saying good-bye.

Pat was saddened at the thought of not seeing Bloomsbury Group Junior again. She would look back on those times as the best of her life. But, she told herself, she must be honest, face up to her deficiency. Not everyone could have the spark of greatness. She would leave tomorrow.

Loud ringing faded Virginius Twyce thankfully away from his nightmare of being chased by gangs of locks swinging lethal lengths of chain. He reached a weaving hand to the alarm clock and stopped its bell. Though halved in volume, the ringing continued. It was, Virginius realized, the telephone.

He got out of bed and quickly made himself presentable —robe on, face rubbed, hair smoothed—before going to the wall instrument and lifting the receiver.

"Hello?

"Oh, good morning, Lady Severn.

"No, your timing is perfect.

"A job?

"Oh.

"Go on, please."

Virginius' stomach began to ache, because he was not able to chew his lips and talk at the same time. "A box. I see. Empty. You want me to get an empty box. About two feet square. Fine. Eleven o'clock. Fine. You can rely on me, Lady Severn. Good morning."

While shivering through a shower and a shave, Virginius dwelled with pleasure on his little mission. There would be no problem getting an empty box. It could be got now on the way to work and taken to the appointed place during his coffee break. Simple. Perfect. Easy as pie.

Dressed, he hurried out. The morning was bleak, gray, smelling of rain. The opening and already open shops were lighted cheerily. Virginius chose a grocer's.

Inside, a schoolboy was being served by a large man who had arms like thighs and hands like bunches of feet. Virginius started to feel less brightly resolute. Big men like that, he thought, were often bullies. They had small minds. They had tiny dinky minds that could see nothing but wrong. Bullies with small minds seized evilly on the most innocuous requests.

Virginius trapped a peck of inner lip between his canines and loosened the grip on his imagination.

"You want an empty box?" the brute asks, frowning, leaning forward over the counter.

"I'm quite willing to pay for it."

"I dare say, mister. Oh, yes. I dare very well say."

"Not too large."

"Oh, no, not *too* large."

"No. Certainly not. Never."

"But large enough to put something *in,* eh?"

"I'm afraid you've got it all wrong, sir. We're not going to put anything in it."

"We? Ah, there's a gang of you."

"No, no, no."

The blackguard pounds his counter. "Don't deny it. I know your kind. You and your empty boxes. Well, mister, you've slipped up this time."

"Terribly sorry."

"You've come to the wrong place, unlucky for you—no! You can't get out. I've just pressed a secret button that locks the door."

"I'm la-late for work."

"Dirty work," the bully says, coming around the counter. "I hate gangsters."

"Clerk, I'm a clerk."

"Gangsters. Should be destroyed. Vermin."

"Leave me alone!" Virginius cries as the beast charges, fists flying.

"Ooh!" Virginius said as he bit through the flesh of his inner lip.

"Beg pardon, sir?"

The grocer was looking at him; the schoolboy was gone. Breathing heavily, Virginius said, "What I want is, er, something you haven't got." He retreated, trying to be casual. "Something so innocent it's incredible."

"Feeling all right, Mr. Twyce?"

Virginius felt the door at his back. "Clerks like me, without friends, always want—" With a sudden jerk he swung around, snatched open the door, flung himself outside, and began to run.

By a circuitous route he ran to the tube station, where he fretted and paced until a train rolled in. Relative calm had come by the time he alighted a few stations on toward town.

He was wiser now. He was not going to give himself away. What people didn't know couldn't hurt him. There was more than one way to get an empty box.

Virginius turned a corner beside a row of shops. He found, as expected, a rear alley. He entered it cautiously after making sure he was not observed. The back yard of almost every shop was a veritable treasure house of boxes, boxes of all shapes and sizes thrown in untidy piles.

He sidled into one of the yards. There was no one in sight. His eyes sorted out a box of the requisite size. He lifted it, delicately, holding his breath, tiptoed back to the alley, and walked off.

His heart was pounding madly at the present danger of being seen in the act of abduction, and his mind was already churning with the next problem: What would he say if later someone stopped him to suspiciously ask, "Is that an empty box you're carrying?"

The bedside lamp fought with the curtains' seep of light for mastery of the room, creating thereby an unattractive grayish pink, reminiscent of salmon paste on porridge.

Jean Quin had no concern to spare for lighting effects. She had her own glow of misery to think of.

Lying across the bed foot, head limply over the edge and arms adangle, Jean was sympathizing with herself for having spent the worst night of her life. She hoped never again to hear the Chancellor's name; and sex, that with her was an extremely sore point. The last thing she would have suspected in civil servants was virility.

Her head ached, her body ached, and time hung heavy on her eyelids. But she told herself she must not let go as she had done before, allow emotion to get the upper hand. There was the mission, that stinking mission.

"Now," said Mr. Percival, "our hero is nearly eight years old."

Jean wearily raised her head to show attentiveness, which act had been her sole contribution to the tête-à-tête for the past several hours. Her bleary, slitted gaze fell on the clock.

She muttered in a hoarse voice, "D'you know what the time is?"

"Yes. No matter."

"You've got to go to work."

"Not today. I'm off. We can spend the whole day together, Ninotchka."

I will not scream, Jean said to herself as she screamed.

"What is it?" jerked Mr. Percival in a high tone.

"Aagh," Jean gaggled, struggling for control and for words. "Out. I've got to go out. I've got to help my mother."

"I see," he said, relaxing. "You've just remembered."

"Yes. Help my mother."

"Very well. We'll go along. But I hope she'll be as interested in my story as you are."

"Help!" wept Jean. "Mother!"

The letter was from Downing Street. Minerva Droplet ripped it open with eager hands and read with disappointed eyes a printed form that said the Chancellor would look into the matter as soon as possible.

Furious, Minerva crumpled the letter into her pocket. It was in reply to one she had considered particularly hot stuff. Her youth and innocence, she felt, were a drawback; even last night's letter, blushingly strong, was probably not enough. What was needed was a good sexy novel to get ideas from. And she would go and buy one right this minute if it weren't for meeting the others. Not that her presence there was vital, she had no part to play, but she couldn't bear the thought of not being mentioned in a future book (". . . everyone was there except Minerva Droplet, the famous painter, whose recent commission by the Sovereign was causing so much comment. The others, feeling lost without their staunch ally, Miss Minerva Droplet, had no heart for the project. If only Minerva Droplet were here, they thought").

Minerva hurried out.

Men fought duels in it, a mob incited by the Reform League battled with police in it, "disabling more than forty for life," Oliver Cromwell driving a coach and six nearly came to grief in it, and when it was for deer, "Duke Casimir killed a barren doe with his piece" in it. Hyde Park.

On this particular day, the area of the park known as Speakers' Corner looked peaceful enough; even dreary. A stranger would never guess that here any person of any degree was free to stir tempers by giving public speech, free to stand up and advocate anything he wished from the suppression of smiling to the hanging of Her Majesty the Queen.

There was a scatter of idle groups. A small one around a man who was calling from his box (Heinz beans, not soap) for the abolition of Shetland ponies. A depressed-looking one of Russian sailors. One of studentish young people with a placard saying Equal Rights for Blacks. One which consisted of Lady Severn, Miss Single, Miss Droplet, Mr. Cease, and Mr. Fourpenny.

Madge Severn, fully out of mourning, had on a plum-colored hat around which two stuffed doves were stalking each other. She was musing on the day's brief newspaper report on the Zero murder. The knife had carried initials, it was now revealed by the police, who further stated that said initials had been traced to the seventh Earl of Choumleighgood 1729-1810. Lady Severn was rather doubtful of the clue's value.

Minerva Droplet was thinking that Mr. Fourpenny was not making a good job of pretending to be not thinking about her, and Sid Fourpenny was wishing Miss Droplet in hell.

Pat Single's thoughts were on escape. She had been packing when the telephone call had come, ordering her to Hyde Park. Not wishing to lie, make some excuse, she had agreed to join. It would not be for long. Then away.

Relentable Cease was wondering if Mr. Twyce had carried out his assignment safely. He ended the wonder when now the equipment supervisor appeared carrying a large cube wrapped in newspaper.

Virginius, pink with triumph, was thinking how well he had done. Not only had he managed to get a box, but he had been shrewd enough to wrap it in newsprint before going to the office, where he answered curious glances with the instant statement that it was a present for his nephew, which he considered pretty clever, seeing as how he had no nephews, only a niece.

Virginius reached his friends, exchanged furtive hellos, and unwrapped the box. His newspaper he carefully put back together, not having read it yet. Paper under his arm, he stood back and saw that the others were looking at the box with expressions of doubt.

"Wrong size?" he groaned.

"I rather think," Lady Severn said with care, touching a forefinger to her chin, "I rather think that what I had in mind was something made of wood."

"Oh."

"Not cardboard."

Wadding his hands, Virginius wailed that he might have known he would do something wrong. Lady Severn told him not to fret, that an expert on silver couldn't be expected to know about *objets* not *d'art,* and it was the thought which counted, while the others all agreed that anyway it was a jolly fine box.

Partly mollified, Virginius took his leave.

"Let us commence," said Lady Severn briskly. "Assistance, please."

The box held firm when Madge was helped into place on its top. She made a striking figure. Pat Single applauded.

"Thank you, Patricia. I suggest we—now what?"

Approaching at a march full of determination were three men. They wore identical green shirts of military cut, brown trousers, broad black belts, and red ties. Two, to the third's rear, carried a banner which stated, "SOCIO-DEMO-FASCINIST LEAGUE."

They stopped. The leader, a short man with no neck, his jowls hiding his collar, said sternly, "You are usurping our position."

"Nonsense, m'lad," Lady Severn said serenely.

"This is our place. It's unofficially reserved. All the regulars know it."

"We are not regulars."

"Be that as it may," the man said loftily, "having now been informed of your error, I request in the name of the Socio-Demo-Fascinist League that you transfer your futile activities elsewhere."

"We'll do nothing of the kind. There's plenty of space."

"But consider, madam, we are Socio-Demo-Fascinists."

"And we are Bloomsbury Group Juniors."

"Never heard of you."

"We're quite well known."

"*We've* been mentioned in the *Daily Mirror*."

"We don't believe in newspapers. The reporters never show up."

"*We* have a royal charter."

"We'll get one soon. We're rather busy at the moment."

The man tutted. "This is all most irrelevant. Are you going to move?"

"Emphatically no."

The man drew an outraged breath and looked as if he might stamp his foot. "You're not being *fair*."

Miss Single felt that he was right. Sid Fourpenny and Mr. Cease, following Lady Severn's lead, folded their arms and appeared implacable. Miss Droplet stepped to the leader and dropped a friendly hand on his shoulder. He turned pale.

Minerva said, "Don't let all this get you upset. There really is plenty of space. And first come first served, you know."

Looking up with cringed eyes, the man offered hesitantly, "Proverbs are infantile philosophy fed to the unschooled by the aristopeasantry."

"You never know," Minerva said. "But look, I'll tell you what, we won't be long and then you can have this place. We'll keep it for you."

The man was keeling a degree under the hand's weight. He stepped back and straightened. The color returned to his face. "You will hear more of this. The Socio-Demo-Fascinists are not so lightly slighted."

Minerva nodded cheerfully. "Good-bye."

The three men marched off, their banner sagging. They gave no sign that they had heard when Sid Fourpenny called out, "And don't you forget it."

"Right," Lady Severn said. "Let us commence. Phase one, please."

The others walked away, spacing themselves, threading the scattered groups, until the area rang with Lady Severn's call of, "Ladies and gentlemen, lend me your ears!" whereupon they swung around with faces aghast with gladness and stalked eagerly back, giving small cries of anticipation.

The ruse had little success. The crowd which assembled before Lady Severn as she again called for ears consisted of Miss Single, Miss Droplet, Mr. Fourpenny, and Mr. Cease. Some people moved pointedly, spitefully, to the Shetland pony abolitionist, the while smiling, as though this is what they had been waiting for. The students were arguing among themselves. Only the Russian sailors showed interest, moving a step closer.

Undismayed, Lady Severn continued loudly, "I am going to tell you about the evil which exists in this country. An evil which, if allowed to grow, could well spread all over the world."

One of the Russian sailors raised his fist and shouted warningly, "I am speaking English."

"A heckler," whispered Lady Severn with joy. "Now we're getting somewhere." Voice raised again, she called, "Who is it who sucks the blood of this nation? Who is it who would like to destroy all art? Who is it who would like to reduce us all to slaves?"

The four-way lid of the cardboard box began to give.

"Who is it," Lady Severn asked, sinking slowly and with dignity, "that has smirched the good name of this country? I'll tell you who, the Chancellor of the Exchequer."

She came to the end of her descent. She was up to the knees in box. Looking down, she said, "Oh, dear. Let's not tell Mr. Twyce."

Relentable Cease assured, "The thing is, it *looks* all right. Still sort of official."

Bravely Lady Severn went on with her speech. After posing more questions, she invited comment. The Russian sailor asked what was being done about the treadmill. Lady Severn said that matter had been solved these many years. The sailor said no and was slapped on the back by his mates.

A man walking a dog dispiritedly joined the group; Lady Severn started again with renewed enthusiasm. "Who is it that has caused untold misery?"

"Well," said Miss Patricia Single, "I don't know about that." Pat felt she should do something to help. If hecklers were needed, she would heckle. Pat also felt that her statement was partially true.

"*I* know," Lady Severn shouted at the recent arrival, who was wandering on. "And who is it that's cruel to animals?"

"I don't believe you," Pat said, half playing heckler, half being herself.

"It's well known."

"Slander."

"Who is it that never helps old ladies across streets?"

Pat was carried away from her playing by her regard for truth, though at the same time feeling sure that, being a simple girl, she must be in the wrong.

She said, "He's probably always helping old ladies."

Madge Severn was also carried away. She had not enjoyed herself so much for ages. "Who put a tax on windows?"

"Charles the First."

The sailor shouted that the feudal system had to depart.

"The Chancellor, that's who taxed windows. And doors. And walls. And iron bars. And prisons. And cages."

"Everything you say is incorrect," snapped Pat, beginning to tremble. She had a red blotch on each cheek.

Lady Severn countered joyously, "You, young lady, whoever you may be, are blinded by insidious propaganda."

"I'm not blinded by anything. I know right from wrong."

"What's right about the Chancellor?"

Reason rendering Pat insensible, she shouted, "What's right about Bloomsbury Group Junior?"

"Everything."

"Lying and cheating to bring about somebody's downfall. Is that right?"

Lady Severn blinked. The others blinked. Miss Droplet hissed, "Sshh."

"Writing love letters to a happily married man," yammered Pat, shedding stored poison. "Chaining yourselves to railings. Trying to corrupt faithful servants."

Lady Severn gaped. The others gaped. Miss Droplet shook Pat's arm, "Shut up, shut up."

"Using foul lies to rouse the rabble. Planning on assass—"

Pat broke off as Lady Severn, making to move forward with reaching, staying hands, began to fall, being as she was boxed of lower legs. She landed with a thud.

Staring down, Pat came back to social reason. What had she been saying? she thought, horrified. Had she let her silly young mind loose among these good, kind, brilliant friends? Yes, she had.

Turning, Pat took off in a stumbling, trembling lope.

Lady Severn was being helped to her feet. She said, spitting out a piece of grass, "Good old Patricia. She played her part very well. We must tell Mrs. Quin. She's made our little venture quite a triumph."

"Victory," said Mr. Cease, wondering why, "is ours."

The Good Samaritan Public House was a large place. Untidy, sagging, it stood on a corner, like a lout. The saloon bar had a dense pack of midday drinkers above whose noise boomed a television set and a piano straight out of a tuner's nightmare, and down on whom gazed smugly, knowing it would win in the end, that omnipresent enemy, the clock.

Because to him men in thick-rimmed spectacles always looked knowledgeable, Jem Gate asked such a one near the door if he knew Portuguese Ned. Jem got a description and a direction. He eased through the crowd and found his man at the bar.

Portuguese Ned was small and dark with sideburns down to his jaw. He wore a foppish pale-gray suit and a regrettable tie. Handkerchief cascading, sly mouth holding a cigar, he looked like a boy's impression of a gangster, or a gangster's impression of a fool.

Glad Lady Severn could not see him now, Jem said, "Killer Watson."

Portuguese Ned looked Jem all over. "Waddle you 'ave to drink?" His accent was a hybrid of Battersea and Brownsville.

"Beer."

The other ordered. "Killer Watson sent you, eh? Well, you know my name, I guess, but I don't want to know yours. We'll call you Mr. X. Okay?"

"Okay."

"Now, you want a job done, eh? A job that's a bit too heavy for the old Killer?"

"Yes."

"You came to the right guy, mate."

"Good."

"Even though I do say it meself, I turn in a first-class job. And I got alibis nobody never 'eard of. And you know what else I got?"

"No."

"Integrity," he said, tapping his breast pocket as if it were full of the stuff. "Integrity."

"Appreciate that."

The drinks came. Portuguese Ned lifted a glass of wine. "Here's mud in your eye, Mr. X."

"Cheers." Jem drank and asked, "Terms?"

"Terms cash. I've been let down in the past with the installment bit. The amount depends on the job. What you got in mind?"

"Permanent."

"Sure thing. That's me specialty."

"No GBH's."

Portuguese Ned looked hurt. "Please, Mr. X. I'm not a tearaway. My work 'as finesse, delicacy, you might even say art."

"Sorry."

"For instance, I can do you a chopped-off hand. Very effective. Lasting value."

Jem shook his head.

"Or a shot-away lower jaw. 'Orrible forever."

Again Jem shook his head. "Permanent."

"They are, they are. With your GBH's and your razor slashings the receiver is up and about in no time. What you want is something that keeps. Like me shattered vertibrae routine."

"Not enough."

"Or I can do you a demolished lung. Ruptured kidney? See, a lot depends on the receiver's occupation—severed leg for a dancer and so on. There's more to this than people think."

"Not enough."

"Or if aforesaid receiver is a male, I can do you an emasculation. Though that comes out kinda expensive like."

"No," Jem said firmly.

"Oh."

"Dead. Receiver dead."

Portuguese Ned raised his black eyebrows. "Ah," he said, not unimpressed, "the Big Bye-Bye, eh? The old Out for the Count bit, eh? Gone and never called me mother, eh?"

"Exactly. Permanent."

"Yes, well, my permanents is in the disability field only. I don't mess with that old curtains stuff."

"Why?"

"I'm not chicken, don't get me wrong. There's plenty of piss and vinegar in this boy, buddy. I'm loaded with guts. I got more guts than Haig's got dimples."

"Then why?"

Portuguese Ned tapped his pocket, which it now appeared contained "Heart."

"Oh?"

"Yeah. I may look tough, and I *am* tough, but inside I'm a whole mess of sentiment. All heart, that's me."

"Too bad."

"Goddam right, mate. It's held me back, I can tell you. I've tried, but it's no go. I couldn't deprive no one of the joys of living."

"Pay well."

"Sure you would, Mr. X. But you've come to the wrong kid."

Jem sighed. He sipped his beer, put down the glass, and asked, "Know anyone?"

Portuguese Ned looked thoughtful. "I might. I might. Yes, if a person was to slip a fiver into my pocket, I just might."

Jem added a five-pound note to the integrity and heart. "Well?"

"Dainty Macklesfield. That's who you want. He's the big rub-out merchant. Does the odd robbery on the side to keep his toes warm, but his real lark is Goodnight Sweet Prince."

"Reliable?"

"Very. Highly recommended."

"Address, please."

Portuguese Ned gave his head a tough shake. "Can't do you his whereabouts, no. He doesn't work that way, not Dainty. Don't call him, he calls you. Tell you what, give me your address, and I'll let him know of your interest."

Jem presented his card. Putting it away, Portuguese Ned said, "By the way, pal, do me a favor, don't mention to Killer Watson that I said anything against GBH's. He can get very belligerent, that one."

Jean Quin undressed slowly, woodenly. Although she had treated herself to a solid eight hours' sleep after finally getting rid of Mr. Percival, she had not yet recovered from her night-long debauch of sex and strong story. She knew she should not have gone out. But the mission, the mission.

When naked, she slipped on her negligee, thudded back to the living room doorway, yawned, and said in a dreary voice, the while lazily gouging a finger in her ear, "Mr. Crippenson, I'm a liar. I knew the bloody window was closed. Fact is, I had to meet you. When I saw you stumbling along Whitehall, something moved inside me. I suppose I felt a burst of heat."

Mr. Crippenson, public relations officer at Number 11, said, "Really?"

"It was love," Jean went on, sounding as though she were describing a piece of stale fish. "Love at first sight."

"Dreadfully sorry, miss. I'm engaged to be married. Thanks all the same."

"Thank *you,*" Jean said, turning away, heading for bed. "Good afternoon."

The area was slummy. As Sid Fourpenny put the wheel lock on his motor-assisted bicycle, peering to see in the growing dusk, he thought it a shame that someone of Miss Single's grace and charm should live in such a district.

Ever since the gathering in Hyde Park, Sid had been thinking of the Group's youngest member. With every hour that passed, her physical attractiveness grew. He had seen her with new eyes when she had heckled Lady Severn, standing there vibrantly, cheeks aglow. He admitted that she was of course no rampant beauty, that her figure was a good way from perfect, that she didn't have a tit about her; but she had *something,* and her obvious passion for him should not be let go to waste. Time was of the essence. He had to make his play now, before the Droplet got to her and warned her off.

Inside, the tenement was dark. Sid had to fumble his way to the stairs and up. And up. And up. He was breathless by the time he reached the top landing.

He found the right door and knocked. He knocked three times. Silence. He tried the handle. The door gave. He entered. Was he expected? Was she waiting for him on the bed?

"Patricia?" he cooed, parting his teeth a roguish fraction as he felt his way into the darkness. He skirted a chair and tripped. Accompanied by the loud crashing of falling crockery, he found himself falling forward. His body met something soft. He grabbed hold. He swung forward and back, forward and back. What he held was loose from the floor, suspended from above. It was like the tackle dummies he had used in army training. However, he knew by the feel that it was not a dummy. He knew that he had found Miss Single.

three

The magistrate's court was a large chilly room one-third filled with disinterested people. Even Lady Severn herself, the sole occupant of the public benches, felt little interest, as little as though she were reading a mystery novel she had read before, being sure of the verdict. Wearing her black half-veil hat, she was attending out of respect; it was like being at a service for Miss Single, whose service proper would have to be boycotted by Bloomsbury Group Junior for fear of implication. There had been a service of sorts yesterday, a day of mourning and suspended operations, at the home of Minerva Droplet, during which Mr. Cease had whistled the six bars so far composed in his Group anthem, and Mr. Fourpenny had recited an ode entitled, "Oh, to Be in Heaven Now That Single's There." Satisfying though the wake had been, Madge Severn was glad of the opportunity to make her sorrow more open, authorized, by attending the inquest.

She had, however, long since stopped listening to the various officials' droning voices, she was disappointed in courtroom drama, and there were no bluebottles buzzing on the windows for her to wax symbolic about. She cradled her bereavement.

Patricia, she thought, was a tragic loss, as was Tony Zero. Both had drifted away within a space of three days. Strange and sad. Never to see their young, honest faces again, never to let them see that they were loved and wanted, and, selfish though it may be, never to cherish their devotion. Luckily the newspapers were not paying much attention, not building the affairs up into something sordid. That would be a terrible epitaph for such purity.

Lady Severn became attentive as she sensed the denouement's approach. She listened impassively to the coroner say, "The verdict of this court is that Patricia Lucinda Single hanged herself while of unsound mind due to her grief over the death of one Antonio Mario Lorenzo Riglianfacchi, whom, according to the note she left and which this court accepts, she stabbed to death two days previously."

The court rose. Lady Severn went out. Unsound mind, she mused. That was of course the explanation of it all. The odd behavior in Hyde Park, the secrecy, not mentioning money when according to the cheerful, inheriting cousin who gave evidence she had been quite well off. On the other hand, coroners nowadays, unless they were hung over or permanently nasty, always urged the unsound mind verdict on their juries, for otherwise the insurance companies would pay nothing. It was good and proper. For one thing the companies were rich, for another no one in his right senses would want people to think he had killed himself while anything but out of his mind.

On the street Madge began to walk. She would find a café and have a snack. It would be like a funeral tea. The event would be properly rounded out.

As she walked, Lady Severn thought how nice it would be if she could get hold of at least one of Patricia's ceramics and one of Tony's designs. They would make nice mementos of beautiful people.

By the time she found a café Madge had given up the idea of mementos. It would be too dangerous. Questions were inevitable. The Group risked exposure, and the cause came before personal desires.

Madge entered the café, sighing. The life of an idealist was sad. She asked for a double order of crumpets.

Eating, she at last turned her mind from tragedy to business. The plan to rid Britain of a monster was not progressing fast enough. They had certainly had successes, but they were moral, not practical, and the monster was still there. Practical, that was the operative word. Bloomsbury Group Junior was not practical. Creative people never were. They needed help. The Group needed help. Outside help. Which of course could not be asked for without great risk. An outsider, if he was not a fool, if he was alive to the . . .

Lady Severn smiled suddenly, excitedly. Alive? Yes, but what if the outsider were dead? What if Bloomsbury Group Junior called for aid from the other world? That was it. Summon up some brilliant organizer who had passed beyond the veil. There were so many. They would be delighted to have the opportunity of getting to work again.

Madge rose and headed for the telephone, listing eagerly all the shades who would be glad to help bring about the Chancellor's destruction: Marcus Aurelius, John Donne, Edgar Wallace, Gandhi. . . .

In Downing Street was gathered the usual motley crowd, augmented today by a mad Anglophile who had his family lined up before him on the curb facing Number 10; staring at the inscrutable façade, they waved Union Jacks, which hung with embarrassment, and broke into occasional, ragged snatches of "Land of Hope and Glory," smiling aside at the sullen policemen, who had warned them twice about their activities and whom they thought were wonderful.

On one of the Whitehall corners, Mrs. Quin had just been joined by Sid Fourpenny. They were offering each other a muttered good-bye, which, change being the unwanted niece of safety, was the new password.

Sid was here to try and pick up the Chancellor's cook. It was the cause he had in mind, he told himself, and had nothing whatever to do with the fact that he was randy to an excruciating degree.

Jean Quin had recovered from her encounter with sleepless virility. Yesterday had been restful. She had had a visit from Green-Jones, frowning gamely, but had got rid of him with an excuse; she had had a telephone call from Mr. Percival, but after making preliminary sounds of interest in Chapter Seven had rested the live receiver and gone back to lounging with a book, returning infrequently to make murmurs of appreciation and finally to tune out his two-hour broadcast, leaving the Chancellor halfway up a tree (coniferous, trunk circumference thirty inches) at the age of eleven and three-quarters. Jean was now ready to take up her work.

"What're you doing here?" she asked.

"That Molly."

"Ah, yes, the cook."

"What time will she leave?"

"No idea, but it won't be now. It's lunchtime, and she's a cook. I fancy she'll be cooking."

Sid grunted. He thought that since he should have realized that for himself, he must still be suffering from shock over the Pat Single affair—finding the body, reading the note in her typewriter, getting out without being seen, making an anonymous telephone call to the police.

"Watch it," Jean hissed. "Here comes a policeman."

Sid glanced at the nearing constable; glanced again; stared.

The officer was a good six inches shorter than regulation height. His uniform sagged at the neck, dangled at the sleeve cuffs, and concertinaed at the ankles. His helmet hid most of his expressionless face. The officer was Relentable Cease.

"Good-bye," he said. "It's me."

"I knew that," unioned Jean and Sid.

"Tell by my voice, of course."

"Mmm."

Mr. Cease looked down himself. "It's a policeman's uniform."

Jean nodded. "I believe you're right."

"Not a real one, mind. That's illegal. But a fairly close facsimile thereof. I rented it from a theatrical costumer's."

Sid Fourpenny, thinking jealously that the other looked pretty smart, clenched out, "So what's your game?"

"It's this plan of mine. I worked on it all day yesterday and half the night. I think I've got it foolproof."

"You're going to arrest the Chancellor," said Jean.

Relentable raised his hidden eyebrows. "This is not funny, Mrs. Quin."

"Sorry."

"This is complex, sophisticated, far-reaching in its implications. Listen, I'll tell you."

The plan of Relentable was that he would gain entry to Number 11 by saying he had a message from Scotland Yard. Inside, he would almost certainly be asked to wait and, while doing so, would ask casually, in the context of a conversation, where the house's water cistern was located. Having learned this, he would overpower the secretary with chloroform and lay him out neatly on the couch so that if people came in he would seem to be having a nap. Next, up to the cistern, into which he would empty a self-concocted cathartic and laxative mixture. Last, before making good his escape, he would hide the bottle, on which was written, "Bought by the Chancellor of the Exchequer."

"You follow?" he said. "Everyone gets deathly sick. If the bottle's found, our friend will be accused of trying to poison the others. Or if it's not found, they'll be so sick that a doctor will order them to take a long sea voyage. Someone can go along and keep slipping my mixture into their food. The Chancellor will resign through incurable illness."

Sid said he was an excellent sailor, and Jean, wondering if her artistic friends could possibly be as simple as they seemed, asked what if the doctor merely ordered Number 11's people to the hospital for a couple of days.

Relentable nodded. "I've been working on that. What I'll probably do is hang about the street for the rest of the day, in mufti and carrying a bag. When someone rushes out of Number 11 shouting for a doctor, I'll say I'm one, go in, take a look, and order an immediate sea voyage."

"Well," Jean said drily, "I suppose it's worth a try."

"Indubitably. And now here I go. I'm quite excited. Goodbye."

Relentable strode diagonally across the road. On the curb he was met by the mustachioed police sergeant, who said, "Hello, your lordship. Going to a fancy dress party?" Crestfallen, Relentable said, "Yes." "Have a nice time." "All right," murmured Relentable and, turning away, left the street.

Fifteen minutes later Jean Quin was alone, Sid having wandered off in a time-passing walk, when out of Number 11 came a man she recognized as the second secretary to the second secretary. She began tuning up her Garbo huskiness.

This she stopped in surprise on seeing that the man, whom she knew to be named Hobbset, was not only headed in her direction but making her his goal, his gaze fixed on hers.

Could he be delivering a note from Green-Jones? she wondered. Or a transcript of Chapter Eight from Mr. Percival?

Hobbset passed close and gave Jean, unmistakably, the eye. Blank of mind and face, she turned. Now out of Downing Street's stern aspect, the man stopped and looked back. He jerked his head, at the same time waving for a cab. Jean tapped herself on the chest. Hobbset nodded impatiently. Limp, Jean approached. She felt, apart from dismay, vague annoyance, as if she had been cheated over a deal in which she was trying to cheat.

"You wanted to talk to me?" she said, resisting the natural urge to tell him he should have remembered to lock the window before he left home.

"Yes. I've seen you here several times." He went on waving for a cab.

Hobbset was a thin, close-eyed man with sunken cheeks and the aesthetic look of a failed priest, one whose only regret was having to leave behind the glee of the confessional.

"Er," Jean said, thinking she had the answer, "has anyone told you about me?"

"Who, for instance?"

"I dunno."

"I didn't need to be told. I saw what you were right away. And it just so happens that you're just what I'm looking for."

Jean told herself that if he asked how much, she would slosh him one.

A taxi drew up. Hobbset opened the door. "Get in."

"Now wait a minute," Jean protested. "I don't even know you."

"I'm John Hobbset, and your name's immaterial. It's what you can do for me that matters. And what I can do for you. Get in."

Jean got in.

The office, modern, pleasantly lighted by tall windows, held four desks of varying sizes, the smallest being the quasi property of Virginius Twyce. One hand nuzzling his thinning hair, the other holding a pen, Virginius was abstractedly adding up a column of figures. His main thoughts were on Patricia Single. They had been there almost constantly for the past twenty-four hours, a mixture of sadness and horror—dwelling on her loss, picturing her gently swinging body. He had been unable to get Pat out of his head. He kept thinking of her, for some odd reason, folded up in a cardboard box. It was terrible, he had thought, the things he was called upon to do for Bloomsbury Group Junior.

The telephone on Virginius's desk rang. Carelessly he picked up the receiver, becoming less careless when he heard, "Lady Severn here."

Crouching low around the receiver, Virginius asked in a voice of stealth, "How did the inquest go?"

"As expected." Lady Severn recited the verdict. "And that's the end of that."

"Yes. Poor Pat. Poor Tony."

"Now there's something I want you to do. Listen."

Virginius listened. His face blanched. He shot a look of disbelief around the office, which had suddenly become full of sinister shadows.

"What?" he hissed into the mouthpiece. "*What* is it you want me to buy?"

The fitted carpeting was deeper than mink, the furniture cooed softly of once having owned whistle-making price tags, the decor was of the stuff that dream magazines are made on, the personal bar had a great deal of the best. Jean Quin reflected that it was a surprisingly luxurious flat for a mere undersecretary to own.

She was sitting in a deep armchair, holding a drink, and puffing nervously on a cigarette. On entering, Hobbset had casually offered her a seat and a cocktail before excusing himself. Jean had horrid visions of his appearing in the doorway dressed only in his underpants and saying, "It was love at first sight."

To her relief, since she found him immensely unattractive, when he did reappear, it was in all his clothes.

He explained, "I've been checking to make sure we weren't followed."

Which was no explanation. Jean naturally said, "I see."

"We don't want anyone knowing our business, do we?"

"Absolutely not."

He poured himself a drink and sat down with a sigh of pleasure. Making conversation, Jean observed that he had a very nice place here.

Hobbset said, "Leaks. They pay well."

Though she looked around surreptitiously for leaks, she could see none and couldn't understand anyway how they would pay anything, unless he sued his landlord.

"Yes," Hobbset went on expansively, "I've had a long and mutually satisfying association with you people."

"I'm so glad."

"There's been a bit of flatness lately. There was nothing solid, in other words."

"Too bad."

"Nothing I could put in to you people."

"Yes," Jean said, wondering how best to react.

"On top of that I lost my best contact. It was an argument

about money. There was an attempt to renew the contact, but one has one's pride. Hence you."

"Indeed. Hence me."

Jean had an idea cooking. She thought that as it seemed positive now he had taken her for a prostitute, she would play along, let him have his pseudocommercial way, but with resistance, which he might mistake for passion. She would then say she was perfectly respectable, he had raped her, she was going straight to the police. Could be he might be blackmailed to heel.

Hobbset said, "I don't think we'll have any discord over the financial aspect, eh?"

"I shouldn't think so."

"Frankly, this is a very lucky break for you."

"Oh?"

"Not many of your lot get a chance of something so big."

Jean looked at him doubtfully. "It's really big, is it?"

"Tremendous. It should be right up your street."

"Street?" asked Jean faintly.

"Yes. You are an all-angles girl, aren't you?"

Jean took a large gulp of alcohol. "Well, er, I'm not sure."

"I don't want just anyone. I want someone who can really handle this."

"I'm not sure," Jean faltered again.

"Look," said Hobbset, clapping his eyes in a brisk manner. "You might as well tell me your name and the name of your newspaper."

"Yes. Newspaper. You knew that."

"I had you pegged the moment I saw you. The trench coat gave you away."

Jean recovered. She understood and began to understand more. "My name's Smith, and I'm with the *Sunday Signal.*"

Hobbset smiled. "The *Signal*'s excellent with this sort of thing."

Jean lifted a blasé eyebrow that was out of Brenda Starr, Ace Reporter. "What exactly have you got, Hobbset?"

He leaned forward. "Miss Smith, this is the greatest smell since anyone's father knew Lloyd George. It will blow the government, as the idiom has it, sky high. It will be the end of the Honorable C of E."

"You really hate him, huh?" Jean asked with relish.

"Heavens, no. He's not a bad fellow. I met him once on the way out to get a shovel of coal. No, this has nothing to do with personalities. Strictly business."

Jean went back to the eyebrow. "Well, let's stick to that, Hobbset."

He paused smilingly before saying, with deliberation, "The Chancellor of the Exchequer, Miss Smith, is involved with another woman. He has, in other words, a mistress."

"That *is* interesting."

"I thought you'd like it. Big enough for you?"

"Very satisfying."

"What I want to know from your editor is how much he'll pay. Also when he intends breaking the story so I can arrange to be off sick at the time."

"What about proof?"

"I have all of that."

"What form does it take, Hobbset? Films? Tapes?"

"Letters. The passionate letters she's been sending him every day. They're opened by me, as is all the mail, and I simply stick them in my pocket."

Jean's Brenda Starr eyebrow sagged. "Would her name happen to be Droplet?"

The man looked sad. "You know?"

Jean downed her drink. "Good afternoon."

It was well after lunch that Sid Fourpenny returned to Downing Street. He waited on the corner. His hair he had combed and recombed to a perfection of unreality, and his Chihuahuan mustache he had accentuated with a lead pencil. He told himself he looked pretty cool.

After a time appeared the woman whom by description he knew to be the cook, Molly. Sid's ardor sank. The description had pertained to height—average; and age—late twenties; and coloring—dark; and complexion—fresh; it made no mention of the fact that the height was mainly torso, the age a gentleman's compliment, the hair coloring came out of a bottle which hadn't been quite large enough, and the complexion was so fresh it was alarming.

This truly would be in the name of the cause, Sid thought as, Molly turning the corner, he started to follow. Not, he told himself, that there was anything wrong with short legs, two-tone hair, or red faces. It was just that, all put together, they didn't make for a good effect. However . . . the cause.

He caught up and fell into step. She looked at him questioningly. "Yes?"

"Miss Molly, I believe."

"Molly O'Neal."

Sid was glad to hear that Molly had a cockney accent. He unclenched his teeth. "That's right. Molly O'Neal."

"You know me?"

"I made it my business to find out your name."

She looked at him severely, craning back her neck. "Here, if you're a reporter." The implication was sufficient.

Sid protested his innocence with every weapon he owned, stopping short only of claiming the inability to read or write. "I'm a butler," he said, pleased with his stroke of genius—butlers always married cooks.

Molly O'Neal chattered about the smallness of the world—she happened to be in service herself—until she remembered. "Here, why'd you find out my name?"

Sid put on a coy look. "I've noticed you before. I always hang around your street in my spare time. I thought I'd like to get to know you, so I asked someone."

The cook's face blushed pale. Sid said his name was Fivepence and that if she had no objections he would walk along with her for a while or to wherever she was going.

"Not going anywhere," Molly said, her color coming tiresomely back. "Only walking. I go for a walk every day between lunch and tea. It's good for you."

"Can I come along then?"

"Suit yourself."

They walked along. Sid gently pumped. He was dulled to

learn that Molly thought her employer the salt of the earth, perked by the news that he was no angel, though.

Molly broke off her talk of doings belowstairs. "I've got to get back now."

"I was just going to ask if you'd like to go to the pictures."

"Can't, Mr. Fivepence. Teatime. But I'll be free tomorrow. The Chancellor won't be home for tea. He's going somewhere nobody knows about."

"Secret, eh?"

"Yes. He had to tell me though, 'cos he knows I'd be as mad as anything if I made tea and he didn't show up."

"Where's he off to then?"

"He's going to make a surprise visit to that exhibition of Swedish war toys at Central Exhibition Hall."

"Fancy that."

The counter in the department store is besieged by customers. The two salesgirls scurry. Some time passes before Virginius is able to get one's attention. He tells her what he wants. She smiles in amused disbelief. "You want a Ouija board? No! I've never heard anything so funny in my life. Did you hear that, sirs and madams? He wants a Ouija board." Everyone looks and laughs, drawing back to better the view. The laughter grows into uncontrolled shrieking; Virginius grows into an unhidable hulk.

Blessedly, a telephone on an adjoining desk rang to chop off Virginius' daydream. Wiping his damp palms, he told himself he was being foolishly melodramatic. Things like that didn't happen. In any case, why should anyone find amusement in the purchase of a Ouija board? It was a perfectly ordinary everyday object. People bought them all the time. They had them under their arms on buses. They asked one another how theirs were getting along these days.

The salesgirl would most likely give a casual nod. "What size?"

"Oh, it doesn't matter."

The girl stares. Her boredom flashes away. "It doesn't matter?"

"Not important, no."

The crowd has suddenly fallen silent. The girl glances around nervously for support. "I—I can't believe it," she says. "You're communicating with the dead and size doesn't matter."

"I'm in a hurry, you see, that's what it is, just give me the first that comes to hand. Any will do."

The girl is aghast. *"Any?"*

The crowd rumbles dangerously. A woman shakes her fist, shouting, "Is that the way to treat your poor dead mother?"

"Your dear mother that helped you in your hour of need," says another, slurping into tears.

A man snarls, "How could you be so cruel?"

Another says, "You should be put in an empty cardboard box."

Virginius tries to explain that he is only looking. He is ignored. The crowd closes in menacingly. There are cries of, "Beast!" "Inhuman swine!" "Beat your old mother, would you?" "Bring back the birch!" From behind, an umbrella crashes down on Virginius' head. He breaks out into the open and begins to run. The raging mob gives chase.

Virginius stood up to end the terrible brain reel. A typist gave him a wary glance. He patted his pockets and sat again.

All nonsense, he told himself. So buying a Ouija board was out of the question.

After a moment he decided to make a board himself, or what constituted one. He set to work cutting up sheets of paper into two-inch squares, on which he would write letters of the alphabet and short prepositions. He worked in a lather of worry: about getting the letters wrong, about being caught at this in the firm's time, about being seen working too industriously by the others.

"I'll be there," Miss Droplet said.

"Good. I've told all the others."

"Should I wear anything special?"

"No, dear."

"Okay, Lady Severn. Bye-bye."

Minerva put down the receiver. She felt in her stomach a presence that could have been either disquietude or excitement or a combination of both. In her mind she felt, beyond question, only the former emotion. What they planned to do later at Bloomsbury was not to her liking. She had no fondness for ghosts and goblins, vampires and headless horsemen and all that sort of thing. She never had been able to read spooky stories. What she liked were strong lights and good old solid reality. Anything to do with the dead, after they were dead—no, thank you.

Which reminded Minerva of Lady Severn's other reason for calling: to report on the morning's inquest. It had turned out right, wrapped up as neat as could be, like something out of a film. Altogether gratifying. The only aspect amiss was the absence at the inquest of Minerva herself. Surely she should have been the one to go. ("Looking lovely in pale black was Miss Droplet, artist of fame, who graciously paused outside the building to sign autographs before going inside to relieve her heartbreak. Miss Droplet was tireless in her efforts for the Cause.")

Which reminded Minerva of her letters. She left the telephone and went to her writing desk. Looking down at what she had so far written, she shook her head. The letter was weak. They had all been weak. Obviously they needed some spark which she did not possess. There had been another reply this morning, a note to say the Chancellor would take up the matter of the drainage with the minister concerned.

Minerva thought it perfectly clear that the horrid man was not really reading the letters, merely glancing, picking out pertinent words. Therefore what she needed were words to arrest the attention. What she needed, in fact, was the dirty book she had promised herself she would buy.

Five minutes later she was descending the stairs.

In the hall she stopped to check her mailbox. Empty.

She heard a scuffling sound. It came from the gloom beyond the staircase. She swung her head. She gasped. She leaped a step backward.

The tall heavy ladder which she had seen falling toward her swept by and hit the floor with an ear-wounding crash.

"Phew," Minerva said, looking into the rear gloom and seeing nothing. "That was close." She went outside.

It was a mild afternoon. Minerva stepped out smartly, tingling with anticipation over her little mission. She felt quite naughty.

Midway to the tube station she got the sensation of being followed. This she thought curious because she had had the same sensation yesterday while out shopping. She looked around and saw only casual pedestrians. And who on earth would want to be following *her?*—aside, she amended hastily, from mashers.

She went on, reached the station, bought a ticket, and was taken down by an escalator. On the platform a dozen people were waiting, looking with offended eyes at the posters of impertinent sweetness and impossible color.

After a moment's dawdling, Minerva stepped to the edge of the platform to peer into the approach tunnel. Trains always came sooner when she watched and willed.

She heard an abrupt rattle of running feet, the sound growing. She turned, curious to see this clot who was racing to catch a train that wasn't there.

As she turned, a man collided with her shoulder. He yelped, staggered on from the meeting, and windmilling his arms, leaned over the drop to the rails.

A train roared in.

Minerva grabbed the man, pulled him back, and pushed him across the platform. "What's the hurry, you silly?"

Hunched inside an overlarge overcoat, a flat cap pulled down low, the man kept on going at a jerky, shaky walk. He didn't look back. He went from sight in an exit passage.

Although Minerva had not seen the fool's face, she felt that he was someone she knew. The feeling came from the way he walked. If she didn't know him, she thought, she had certainly seen him before.

The train doors hissed open. Minerva got aboard and forgot the incident.

The bookshop she chose in Soho was small and dirty. The perfect place, Minerva thought with amusement, to buy a dirty little book. ("Miss Droplet, widely known for her artistic skill, was known also by her friends for her lightning wit.")

Inside, there was one customer, and at the moment of her entry he shot the book he was reading up to his eyes and held it an inch from his face. Minerva tutted. The vanity of some people, she thought, they *wouldn't* wear spectacles. But the man's action was encouraging. The books here certainly seemed to grab the eye.

She asked for *Gang-Bang Gal,* paid, and left.

Miss Droplet left. Sid Fourpenny lowered the book from his face, slowly. His mouth drooped. He was immensely surprised. Minerva Droplet, here of all places, buying the victim of a recent book burning. She didn't seem the type. You'd think she would only read stories about big jolly girls playing hockey. Maybe he'd made a mistake about old Min, letting himself be put off by her big lethal hands.

Sid shook his head absently when the shop proprietor asked if he liked the book, put it back on the counter, and wandered out. Retreating in the distance was the form of Miss Droplet.

As he watched, another form began to block his view. A male form. A form he knew.

Sid's eyes opened creakingly wide—he was receiving his second immense surprise of the afternoon. Walking a short way behind Minerva Droplet was one he recognized, despite lack of uniform, as the Socio-Demo-Fascinist from Hyde Park, the man whose place the Group had stolen.

Sid stood gaping until the pair had gone from sight. Dazedly he began to walk. It was some minutes before his mind was able to tick over rationally and coolly. The thoughts came fast.

Miss Droplet had been peculiarly successful in handling the SDF leader the other day. A lot of things were peculiar. Tony and Pat. Miss Droplet had put the spoke in with Mrs.

Quin. Miss Droplet was forever chasing him and trying to get real friendly. Miss Droplet had been mad-eager when, after their meeting through his newspaper ad, he suggested taking her along to Bloomsbury.

Sid's thoughts swirled around until their vortex sucked down a question: Was Miss Droplet a spy for another organization?

Everyone was on time for the meeting at Lady Severn's. Out of respect for those who had passed on, voices were kept low as members talked of their individual progress.

Jem Gate, who had spent the day at his yard and was uneasy to be away from it now, expecting at any time a visit from Dainty Macklesfield, said that he had nothing yet to report on his secret project. Mrs. Quin gave a bowdlerized version of her adventures thus far and admitted she had accomplished little. Minerva Droplet, blushing, said she was turning out some particularly strong letters, which, if and when they came to light, would not only spell the Chancellor's end but force him to flee to Paris. Mr. Cease reported success in getting a rebate from the theatrical costumer's for returning the police uniform so early.

Sid Fourpenny's report was the hit of the evening's overture.

Sid had no qualms about telling in the presence of Miss Droplet what he had learned from Molly O'Neal of the Chancellor's secret plans. He figured that here was a perfect way to get proof of her duplicity. If any Socio-Demo-Fascinists showed up at Central Exhibition Hall tomorrow, their knowledge of the Chancellor's visit could have come only from Minerva.

There being few things more frightening than success, Sid Fourpenny sat down from his announcement in a shower of smiles and murmurs bred of fear. He didn't fail to note that Minerva looked especially put out.

"This news," said Lady Severn, "is most opportune. With the expert I am going to call in, we should be able to turn the occasion to great advantage."

Mr. Cease frowned. "You're calling in an expert?"

"Perhaps I should say call *upon* or call *up*."

"But an outsider."

"Dead, alas. I refer to Machiavelli."

"Politics?" Jem Gate asked, sitting up.

"Of course not, Mr. Gate. Do be careful what you say."

Jem flushed. "Sorry."

"Intrigue, that's why we want this gentleman. He can help us with his vast knowledge of sly planning. If you will get things ready, Mr. Twyce?"

Virginius took the cloth off a circular table and started to set out his slips of paper, the while explaining that as there had been a run of late on Ouija boards in London he had been unable to buy one anywhere. Miss Droplet said the papers were very sweet.

Following Lady Severn's orders, everyone brought a chair to the table except Relentable Cease, who sat apart with pad and pencil to take down messages. An upturned glass was placed in the ring of letters and words. Lady Severn switched off lights, leaving only one low-power lamp, before sitting at the table herself. The right-hand forefingers of the six séancers were placed on the upturned glass.

"Now," the hostess said in a hushed voice, "concentrate."

Minerva Droplet said tightly, "If anything happens, I shall scream."

"Concentrate."

The gathering settled. Lady Severn leaned forward, whispering, "We are calling on Mr. Machiavelli."

The glass made no move.

"Are you there? Is anyone there?"

No movement.

"Do you have a message for us?"

Nothing.

Madge Severn sighed. "Oh, dear, I seem to be no good at this. What a shame. I had so hoped—"

The glass jerked. Stared at by every eye it described a small circle. It swooped to the side and began to peck at letters.

Mrs. Quin called out, *"H . . . e . . . l . . . l . . . o."*

The glass slid to a stop. The participants, excepting Miss Droplet, exchanged bright, appreciative glances.

"Hello, Mr. Machiavelli," said Lady Severn.

The glass moved again, going to *NO*.

Virginius Twyce said, "Er, I think he was a prince. Perhaps you shouldn't call him mister."

"Hello, Your Highness."

No.

"Are you not Prince Machiavelli?"

No.

"Who are you, please?"

The glass tacked and swooped across the table. Jean Quin called out the letters. Mr. Cease wrote them down. When the glass stopped, he read out in a small voice, "Single."

Around the table ran a gasp. Although most had already formed a word from the letters, that word only became a name when spoken aloud.

Lady Severn glanced at every shocked face before asking, "Are you Patricia?"

Yes.

The room was still. The looks exchanged now were of disbelief, fear, or uneasiness.

Jean Quin said, "I suggest the contact should prove itself by giving the new password."

Good-bye spelled the glass.

Minerva Droplet drew a shivery breath. "Listen," she said, "I think we'd better not go on."

Virginius Twyce stopped gnawing his lip to say, "I agree."

"I don't care for this lark myself," Sid Fourpenny said. Sweat was gathering under his eyes.

Minerva withdrew her arm. "Right, that's agreed."

"*Wait* a minute," said Madge Severn. "What is there to be afraid of?"

"I'm not afraid. I think it's silly, that's all."

Virginius: "I agree."

"But if there's a chance of it's helping our cause," Lady Severn persuaded.

"Can't hurt try," Jem Gate said.

Minerva swallowed heavily, bobbing her head. "I'll do the writing then."

"No, no," said Mr. Cease. "This is my job."

"Oh, come on, Droplet," Jean Quin gruffly urged. "We're wasting time."

With reluctance, Minerva returned her finger to the glass. "I don't like it. I hope you all remember that."

"Sshh." Lady Severn hissed. "Concentrate. Everyone."

They concentrated. Jean Quin asked, "Pat, were you very much in love with Tony?"

No.

"Only a bit?"

No.

"You *were* having an affair with him, weren't you?"

No.

Mrs. Quin felt disillusioned. Everyone watched the immobile glass. Virginius Twyce said that that seemed to be that, so now they should finish.

Lady Severn asked, "Did you stab Tony, Patricia?"

No spelled the glass. It began to circle, as though impatiently.

"Have you a message for us, dear?"

The glass shot to a letter, to another, to another. It went on zagging and crossing. Its squeak on the table was the room's only sound, apart from Mrs. Quin's repeating of the letters. The six forefingers sweated, the six arms ached. Mr. Cease scribbled at a furious pace. Everyone was relieved when at last the glass came to a halt.

Lady Severn leaned back, pulled a handkerchief from her sleeve, and dabbed at her damp face. "What did she say, Relentable?"

"One moment, please. I'm breaking it into words and sentences."

"It's probably advice," Jean Quin said. "No doubt over there they know everything." She added, "Not that I believe in all this."

Jem shrugged. "Never know."

"Load of rubbish, if you ask me," said Sid Fourpenny, his voice unsteady.

Virginius gave a nervous series of nods. "I agree."

"Ready," Mr. Cease said. He cleared his throat and began to read.

"I was not afraid when I opened the door and found my friend there. Why should I have been? A friend is a friend. We had spent many hours together. I had of course acted foolishly that day but nothing really. So I suspected nothing. It was quite well done as a matter of fact. When I felt the hands come from behind onto my shoulders, I thought it a gesture of friendship, of understanding. By the time I realized otherwise it was too late to cry out."

"Stop it!" snapped Minerva Droplet. "It's beastly, evil."

"I couldn't agree more," Virginius said.

Mr. Cease offered, "I'll not read the rest of it, if you like."

Lady Severn commanded, "Go on, Relentable. Let us hear it all."

Mr. Cease read, *"The hands came around my neck and started to squeeze. The pain wasn't bad. I suppose there are worse ways to die. I can think of lots. But it did feel uncomfortable, and my head seemed to be on the point of exploding. Anyway it was soon over. I was dead."*

Relentable paused. He looked pale and shaken, though no more so than any of the others. When Lady Severn gestured, he went on.

"After I was dead, my friend produced a piece of rope, looped it around my neck, and drew me up to the rafters. Being light, I was easy to handle. Typing out the note on my machine took only a minute, and great care was observed as to the leaving of fingerprints. In fact the whole thing was very well done. Altogether what one would expect from a member of Bloomsbury Group Junior."

Mr. Cease looked up from the pad. "That's all."

The gathering shuffled, sighed, coughed, glanced everywhere except at one another. Everyone waited for someone else to speak. The first was Lady Severn.

Hesitantly, she said, "Shouldn't we ask, er, who?"

Virginius drew back. "Who what?"

"Who the friend was."

"Really," Jean Quin said. "You're not taking any notice of this, are you?"

"No, no, no, assuredly no."

Miss Droplet reached forward a shaky hand and swept the papers from the table while Jean grabbed the writing pad, took it to the hearth, and gave it to the flames, saying, "Disgusting slander."

Virginius Twyce ventured, "It's a good thing nobody believes in this nonsense."

"Right," Sid Fourpenny said. "Right."

"Ditto," said Jem.

Lady Severn clapped her hands. "I've just remembered," she smiled. "That Machiavelli, he was a rotter, always up to no good."

Virginius again gave a series of nods, now keen. "True, very true, yes."

"Isn't it just like the cad to play an evil trick like that, try and sow discord."

"Yes. True."

"Now we'll forget all about it. We'll have a nice cup of tea and get down to planning tomorrow's demolition of the Chancellor." At the door she paused. "Wasn't it lucky that we remembered what a swine the prince was?"

"Another success for the Group," murmured Mr. Cease, looking gray and unhappy.

Later that night, wearing a thick overcoat and a balaclava helmet, Jem Gate was at work in his yard, under floodlights, chipping at a slab of stone. He didn't mind working overtime when it was for the Cause.

But all this nonsense, he thought, could be ended if only he could make contact with the mysterious Dainty Macklesfield.

Jem stayed his hammer to look over toward the road. Several times since his interview with Portuguese Ned he had seen loiterers, who, once knowing themselves seen, ceased to loiter and smartly left. He thought it not unlikely that they were Macklesfield's men, checking. On the other hand the men could have been simply loitering, with or without intent. He would just have to go on waiting. He hoped it wouldn't be too long. The situation was beginning to get on his nerves. His work was suffering. Only this afternoon he had misjudged a strike and rendered an angel's right breast nippleless. Now he would have to reduce the whole protuberance to create another nipple, then match up the left breast, making for a very poor bosom. People didn't like their angels flat-chested. He might even have to lower the price.

Jem sighed and went back to chipping. Take care, he cautioned himself; an imperfection on this job could have nasty consequences.

The telephone rang in Jem's cottage. He downed tools and went to answer, hearing, "Is that Mr. Gate?"

"Right."

"This is Scotland Yard."

Jem's throat, chest, belly, and buttocks grabbed to tightness. He took a deep breath and said a calm-sounding, "Yes?"

"We've taken over from the divisional police, see. We're on the job now."

"Don't see."

"What I want to know is, have you been contacted by Dainty Macklesfield yet?"

"Who?"

"Dainty Macklesfield, the professional exterminator."

"Unknown," said Jem, "to me."

"Maybe you haven't met him, but you do know whom I'm talking about."

"No."

"Aren't you the one who's been trying to trap him for us?"

Jem relaxed with both relief and pleasure. He was being tested. "Wrong number," he said and put down the receiver. Renewed in confidence, he went outside. Soon he would meet Mr. Macklesfield.

* * *

Many hours later morning light was entering with reluctance a fetid bed-sitter.

The room was like the stage set of a kitchen-sink drama whose company couldn't afford a decent set. Indeed, the sink itself was cracked. Almost everything was cracked. What lacked the consistency to crack was bent, creased, rotted, frayed, or just plain broken. Even the aspidistra in the window looked sick. The room was the kind that Dickens might have invented and in which Oscar Wilde might have been found dead. Being found dead in, an observer would be forgiven for thinking, was about all the room was good for.

Relentable Cease only appeared to be dead. Face paler than normal, closed eyes ringed with dark, he lay in bed with his arms folded across his chest—the last attitude out of habit, for he had long believed that when he died, it would be in his sleep, and he wanted to give as little trouble as possible.

However, there had been no sleep for Relentable during the night now ended. His mind had refused to rest. While he had lain there quietly, not pacing or brow thumping as others might, he had been sorely troubled.

The problem was Patricia Single. Again and again he had relived the scene at Lady Severn's, with himself performing what you could say amounted to automatic writing. He felt that the message was true, its source genuine. That was bad enough. What worsened matters was that as stenographer it had seemed that he was being addressed personally. His conscience ached.

Despite a certain flippancy in Pat's message, which could have been a fault in transmission, he felt that it was more than a mere relating of events; it amounted in essence to a cry for help. Pat wanted her death avenged.

Relentable sighed. He thought of the part of the message which disturbed him most: the statement that the killer was a member of Bloomsbury Group Junior. This he found hard to credit. For the dozenth time he pictured each member and tried to look at him with objective eyes. He made up his mind. No, none of them could be guilty, they were too fine, decent, gentle, and certainly he himself was not responsible. That part of the message must be wrong, *was* wrong. It had come right at the end, possibly when the connection was fading. It was another fault in transmission.

Yet that did not help him greatly. If he did what his conscience begged—reported the knowledge to the authorities—the Group would still become involved, and at the present time that could be dangerous. What was he going to do?

Relentable sighed again and with the question still unresolved fell at last into a fitful sleep.

Virginius Twyce could hardly rouse himself to give decent thanks when one of the office girls brought him a cup of tea. His mood was grumpy. He felt that he was receiving unfair treatment. After all the dangerous missions he had been handed and had pulled off, he was being left out of a fun thing—going to Central Exhibition Hall. It had been Mr. Fourpenny's doing, with his, "You've got to go to work." True enough, there was work, but he could have gotten away and, in fact, could yet get away. He could make some excuse to leave early and then go along to CEH, not necessarily with the others, just to *be* there. It was an idea. Yes, it was an idea.

Virginius got up and thanked the office girl profusely for bringing him his tea.

The bedroom had one small wardrobe for clothes and two large wardrobes for hats. The smaller cabinet was now empty, its contents strewn and entangled on the bed like a couturier's nightmare of an orgy. It had taken a long time, but Lady Severn had finally decided on the right garment: a green-velvet evening gown which had the correct appearance of panic and the needed room in the waist.

She put the gown on, tugging it down over the pillow she had strapped to her stomach. Fastening the nape catch, she faced a mirror.

The effect, she thought dully, was not quite what she had

hoped. Was it the way her décolletage was pulled below her chest? Was it that pregnant women didn't go in for evening gowns? Was it the deep, strap-drawn depression across the middle of her stomach? though if so, she could always maintain that the division meant twins.

Madge Severn shook her head, as if reproving herself for trying to avoid the issue. Mirrors told the truth, she mused. Manifestly she was a little, a bit, a *mite* too old to be with child. It would be seen to be an act. If she did call at Number 11 to make a scene about the Chancellor not doing his duty by her, she would no doubt be scorned. So the idea was out. And it had seemed so good.

Madge continued to gaze in the mirror, not entirely displeased with her reflection. She had always been taken with the notion of motherhood. In truth, she admitted, it was more than being taken with, it had been for many years an all-consuming crave for. But she had been doomed to unfulfillment.

She gazed on, head slanted, eyes growing misty. Then she turned away with a businesslike snap and began to change back into her tweed suit.

She told herself she was wrong. Her ambition had been fulfilled. She had the Group, her artists, who in their innocence and unworldliness were exactly like children. And she couldn't love them more if her own children they were. They could be naughty at times, of course, and had to be disciplined, but all things considered, no mother could wish for a finer, more devoted family. She was a lucky woman. She would have to pray that there were no more bereavements. Her heart was already close to breaking.

"The Right Honorable Chancellor of the Exchequer begs to inform you that you are not eligible for relief under the Marshall Plan."

Minerva Droplet snorted. She thrust the letter back in its envelope and started upstairs. She was in no mood to take the latest reply lightly, philosophically. She was grieved at being left out of the team that was going to Central Exhibition Hall. They had no right to treat her this way after all the work she had done for the cause, slaving at love letters. They would be sorry. Things would be sure to go wrong if she wasn't there. Which would serve them right. They would make a mess of the assignment, and it would be funny. A scream. In fact it might be worth watching. In fact there was nothing to stop her going there to watch. No one had said she should stay away, in fact.

Minerva came into her flat. Pacing as she thought, her eyes fell on *Gang-Bang Gal*. As yet she had not been able to get up enough courage to open the book. She had firmly decided that she would start to read it this afternoon, suffer its horrors while the others were enjoying themselves at CEH. Knowing how terrible the book would be, her groin tingled.

She was too noble, thought Minerva. She gave too much of herself. What she should do was spin a coin to choose between the pleasure of watching the others or the pleas—the pain of reading a disgusting book. ("Droplet, known internationally by only her surname, was sorely tried by the tasks she elected to do for the Group.")

True, true, hummed Minerva as she went in search of a penny.

At three o'clock that afternoon the turnstiles of Central Exhibition Hall were clicking languidly. They were watched over by a policeman hopeful of leapers, a commissionaire hopeful of tippers, and a St. John Ambulance man hopeful of fainters.

Extra alertness came to their bearing when they were advanced upon by a group which contained some likely prospects: an older woman looking both infirm and wealthy, an older man looking like excellent faint material, a spivish type who had that turnstile-leaping look about him, a man of between years whose eyes were kind, tippish, and a woman looking mysterious enough to be anything larcenous, attractive enough to be generous, and feminine enough to take suddenly ill and be in need of pulse feeling and garment loosening.

Hope sank. The five arrivals marched through without flop, tip, or jump. The guardians, who seconds ago had been lauding a television play, went back to it for a sneering reappraisal.

Once out of sight of the turnstiles, Mr. Cease, Mr. Fourpenny, Mr. Gate, and Mrs. Quin stopped, gathering around Lady Severn, who said, "I think it was a mistake for us to enter together."

Sid nodded shrewdly. "See the way they gave us the once-over?"

"They'll certainly remember us," Mr. Cease said.

"More importantly," pointed out Jean Quin, "they'll remember that one of us was carrying the blunt instrument."

The blunt instrument was a piece of stone chipped and ground by Jem Gate into the shape of a Gladstone bag. He was proud of it. It was most realistic. He was saddened when Lady Severn said, touching her hat, which featured a nest with three eggs, "Perhaps we had better call off Plan One and proceed with Plan Two."

Jem left his sculpting in a dark corner and rejoined the others. They moved on.

Plan One was to drop the stone on the Chancellor's head. Plan Two was less complex. If successful, if everyone played his part well, if the dozen aspects which could go wrong went right, it would cause an international incident and lose the C of E his job.

The Group walked along aisles sided with the Swedish war toys: cannons and tanks that blew up; ambulances that broke down; wounded soldiers that leaked bloodlike oil; active soldiers that charged with big smiles; dead soldiers that held white flags; jungle villages which, made of asbestos, could be sprayed with a fuel and burned over and over again.

Lady Severn said, looking upward, "I have just noticed there is no upper level in this exhibition hall. We could not have dropped the stone. Another mark for us, eh, Mr. Cease?"

Relentable merely grunted. Having been here before, he had known there was no balcony. Last night when plans were being discussed, he supposed he must have been involved with his problem. He still was. Only more so. As time passed, the disease in his conscience grew more malignant.

The Group stopped. Ahead stood a snack bar advertising Swedish delicacies and tended by two blue-eyed blondes. The counter, formed in a square, was lined with munching customers.

"Plan Two," Lady Severn said. "Forward, Mrs. Quin."

Jean marched to the snack bar, to its farther side counter. "Coffee, please," she told one of the blondes and continued loudly, "I'm a reporter. The *Daily Record.* I'm here to cover the surprise visit of the Chancellor of the Exchequer."

Having now got the attention of the other customers, she exclaimed, pointing, "Why, here he comes now." As everyone looked, she added, "In disguise naturally."

Surrounded by Lady Severn, Mr. Gate, and Mr. Cease, who were trying to look like a politician's entourage, Sid Fourpenny strode to the counter, the while making furtive adjustments to his dark spectacles and cap.

There was a hum of appreciation from the customers.

"Swedish coffee and a piece of that Swedish cake," Sid ordered, extremely through his teeth.

Until his order arrived, Sid muttered quiet gibberish to Lady Severn, who responded with, "Yes, Chancellor," "No, Chancellor."

On the counter before Sid was placed cake and coffee. He tasted the drink, spat it onto the floor, and said, "Horrible!" The customers gasped. He put a piece of cake in his mouth, spat it out, and said, "Vile!" The customers oooed. The blondes drew deep breaths.

"Whatever can be amiss, Chancellor of the Exchequer?" cried Lady Severn.

"All this Swedish food is rotten!"

"Steady, mate," snarled one of the delicate blue-eyed blondes, whose cockney accent was thick enough to tie in a bow or muffle a bell. "Me mum made all this gear."

" 'It 'im, Alice," urged the other girl.

"Is your mother Swedish?" Sid asked.

"Me *mum? Swedish?* You've got to be *joking.*"

"Go on, Alice, 'it 'im."

Lady Severn hissed. "Retreat."

The four imposters turned away and walked after Jean Quin, who was already in retreat. Answering a raucous command, Sid Fourpenny had to lope back cowed of head to pay for his cake and coffee.

Shaken, the five regrouped by a model of a crashed airplane. Mrs. Quin observed that Plan Two seemed to have misfired.

"Oh, I don't know," Lady Severn said. "As the offerings are not really Swedish, I think we came off rather well, don't you, Mr. Cease?"

Relentable grunted.

"Certainly," said Lady Severn. "And now I suggest we proceed with Plan Three."

"Agreed," said the others.

"Then let us find the correct place and make preparations."

They moved off, looking for the exhibit of which the BBC would be doing a telecast and which, by an odd coincidence, would be visited at the same time by the Chancellor of the Exchequer.

Plan Three was rather sophisticated. They would lead off the stand's microphone out of sight and replace it with a dummy; when the Chancellor spoke, one of the Group would speak simultaneously into the real mike and pour vilification on everything British, beginning with toys and ending with love of dogs. It would be the end of the Chancellor's political life.

The conspirators assembled before the stand with a dozen other loiterers. A television camera stood waiting; its crew walked in busy circles, giving one another orders or urgent whispers. The team in charge of the exhibit—a submarine that could sink without a trace—wandered around practicing smiles and not touching their makeup. Every few minutes one of the crew or the team would go to the microphone and say "One-two-three," and the people watching would nudge one another.

The Group formed a huddle. Mrs. Quin spoke the single thought, "There's too many people about."

They pondered the problem.

Jem Gate said, "Diversion."

"Exactly." Lady Severn touched Jem's arm in gratitude.

"I could scream," Jean offered. "Go a few stands away and give a great yell. Everyone'd come running."

Jem shook his head. "Might not."

Madge Severn agreed. "Anyway, it would be risky. They might show you on TV."

Sid Fourpenny said, "How about darkness? You know, darkness. We switch off all the lights in the hall . . ."

"And," took over Lady Severn, "under cover of darkness we change the mikes."

Jean looked at her with admiration. "Perfect idea."

Mr. Cease said drearily, "I know where the mains are. Been here many times."

"Right. You go and switch off. The rest of us will get in position."

Relentable moved away. He walked in a plod. He had no enthusiasm for the job. Not that he was against it or the main project; he had a larger burden to carry; in point, the problem of whether or not he should report Pat Single's message to the authorities. He had explained his dilemma to a Group member while waiting outside for the others to arrive, hoping for guidance. He had met with only indifference. He would have to make the decision himself.

At the side of the hall he entered a dim passage. Picking his way through clutter, he went to concrete steps and down to another passage, this dimmer. He stopped abruptly on hearing above the sound of footsteps.

A moment after he had stopped, the footsteps also stopped. He shrugged and went on.

He could always say he was looking for the washrooms,

he thought as he turned a corner; there was nothing to worry about. Nothing compared to what he already had. Pat Single gave him no rest. The worry might seem a paradox with what they were trying to accomplish, but a political killing was one thing and a personal killing another.

He came to a door marked "KEEP OUT." He went in. The facing wall of the small room was festooned with wires, cables, and dials arranged around three large switches.

Footsteps sounded in the passage outside. Relentable closed the door and shot a bolt. He was heading for the switches when the footsteps halted and a voice asked, "Are you in there, Mr. Cease?"

Relentable opened the door. "Hello. What're you doing here?"

"I came to help."

"It's not much of a problem. I wish my other were as small."

"Oh?"

"Patricia. That message."

"Ah."

"I can't stop thinking about it."

"Got a match?"

"What? Oh, yes." Relentable produced matches and struck a light. "I feel that I should do this for Patricia. I'm sure I'll have to do it sooner or later."

"These three switches down?"

"Yes," Relentable said absently. The room light went out. He went on, "In fact I'll probably go along and do it after we're finished here."

"I see."

In the glow of his match flame Relentable watched without interest as the other detached a cable from its connection. "Not that I think for a moment that any of the Group is involved."

"Of course not."

"It just sounded that way. Ambiguous."

"Quite."

"Oh, thanks," Relentable said, taking the wires of the cable end as it was handed him. "What's this for?"

"You'll see."

"Hurry up. The match is almost out."

"I'll switch on then."

"Not while I'm holding—"

four

"Alas, poor Mr. Cease, we knew him well, a fellow of infinite jest."

Lady Severn poked a handkerchief under the half veil of her mourning hat and dried the last of her tears. She would cry no more. She had been in tears most of the night. Because, being of an age, she had shared with Relentable Cease the sadness of memory, of things that had been, she felt his loss more stridently than the passing of Miss Single or Tony Zero.

"He has gone to lay his lovely head on heaven's breast."

Pat and Tony were also in the mind of Minerva Droplet, mitigating her sorrow. It would be nice for Mr. Cease to have company. They could all be artistic together.

"Therefore never send to know for whom an angel sings."

Jem Gate nodded. There was a good idea. As soon as the mission was over and his time more his own, he would carve for poor old Relentable an angel, long-haired and holding a baton, and have it delivered anonymously.

"With Cease there, it would scorn to change its place with kings."

Virginius Twyce had both lips inside his mouth—no easy feat—and a hand on the lump in his throat. Even if you hadn't liked a person, he thought, though as it happened he had liked Mr. Cease, these orations were always terribly emotional.

"Never was so much done by one Cease for so few."

Jean Quin allowed the tears to run down her face unchecked. She was much upset. Of all the members of Bloomsbury Group Junior she had considered Relentable the sweetest.

"The only thing we have to fear is Cease himself," Sid Fourpenny said in conclusion, "being sad on the dust and silence of the upper shelf."

Everyone sighed.

It was gray and early the following day. The funeral service, at Miss Droplet's, brought to an end the mourning period, which had been fixed at only overnight because of haste. There was no time for the Group to indulge its sorrow. The cause must be hurried along. Too much time had been wasted on attempted niceties. All were agreed that the answer was assassination pure and simple, the more immediate the better. No more nonsense.

The Chancellor of the Exchequer had not, after all, made a surprise visit to the exhibition, which cast no shadows on Sid Fourpenny's ability as a gleaner of information. Mrs. Quin had learned in a telephone call to one of her secretary-lovers that at the present time, with the Chancellor making budget allowances for a new bomber, he could not afford to associate with neutralists. In the event, it was just as well. During the panic of sudden darkness nothing had been accomplished with the microphones, and Lady Severn had been punched on the ear.

"It still hurts," she said, after a suitable silence following the poem. "But it is as nothing compared to the pain inside."

Jean Quin got out a compact and began to repair her makeup. "Poor old boy," she said briskly.

Jem Gate lifted his chin. "Martyr."

"Yes," Virginius Twyce said, moving toward the door, "a martyr to the Cause."

Sid scuffed his toe sulkily. "I don't suppose anyone liked my composition."

Everyone enthused about his composition. Jem Gate

slapped him on the back. Sid admitted that it wasn't a bad old composition really.

Lady Severn: "It is a perfect memorial to one who gave his life in such a valiant way."

"I wonder how it happened," said Miss Droplet, who was actually wondering if Sid Fourpenny had noticed her new dress with the buttons down the front and the bows on the hem.

Mrs. Quin put away her compact. "It said in this morning's paper that he must have gotten lost and was passing the room when the lights fused, so went in to try and be helpful. A lucky assumption for us."

Lady Severn said, "And how sweet of the musicians' union to be taking care of the funeral arrangements."

Mr. Twyce gave the door handle a nervous rattle. "I must go, if you'll pardon me for mentioning it. I'm half an hour late already."

Lady Severn gave a gracious wave. "Very well, Virginius. Don't forget your task. And all of us, let us think hard. Think Assassination."

The wake was over.

Madge Severn declined the offer of a lift either in Jem Gate's truck or on Sid Fourpenny's motor-assisted bicycle, saying she preferred to walk while she thought, and she was going to think Assassination like anything.

Leaving the others, Madge set off at a grave, steady pace, hands aftly clasped. Her determination to see the Chancellor of the Exchequer in his grave was now strengthened. Had he not, she mused, been an accessory before the fact in connection with the death of Relentable Cease? Yes. He had not known, indeed, of Relentable's existence and possibly knew nothing of his passing, but it was on account of the Chancellor that Relentable had been killed; that was beyond denial, an absolute truth. If it had not been for the Chancellor, Relentable would be alive today. The Chancellor was to blame.

Finished with logic, Madge went on to the hows and wheres

of destruction. Running him down with a car was out, because he never seemed to walk anywhere. Relentable had already tried the poisoning angle—though something might be developed from Sid Fourpenny's association with the cook, and one could always send by post a ground-glass pie. Beheading held a certain charm but would be difficult to arrange. Also difficult to set up were drowning, falling out of a window, and choking on a collar stud. Blunt instruments had been a flop. There was a possibility of frightening the man to death, perhaps by sending Mrs. Quin in to act as a ghost, but being an insensitive brute, the only result could be his putting an extra tax on haunted houses, for their entertainment value. Loosing deadly snakes in Number 11 had the same fault as the other poisoning ideas, one couldn't be sure of getting the right person without harming others, as was true of burning the house down or blowing it up. Electrocution, of course, was the ideal method, sort of poetic justice, but how to get him into Central Exhibition Hall?

Madge Severn shook her head. The task was not going to be easy. She hoped the others would come up with an idea, perhaps contiguous to Virginius Twyce's purchase, though she would prefer something of a less barbaric nature.

She paced on, thinking hard. Gas? Hatchet? Disemboweling? Gangrene?

The small car turned the corner after the Rolls Royce. Jem Gate was sure now that he was being tailed. He took another turn. The car followed. Deciding to remove all doubt, Jem brought his Rolls to a stop by the curb. The car went on by for fifty yards before also stopping. Doubt removed.

When the car had passed, Jem had glimpsed the passengers: two males and a female. None of them now made a move to get out.

Jem himself got out. He was calm. He felt sure he knew what the trio was playing at.

He turned back and began to stroll. Without looking behind he strolled until he came to a coffee bar. He went in. The place, seedy and noisome, was empty apart from the man behind the counter, who was fat-faced almost to the point of eyelessness.

Jem sat on a stool, ordered tea. He was stirring his cup when the door opened and another customer came in. Looking sidelong, Jem saw a girl with a mass of red hair falling to the shoulders of her fur coat. She was fiercely pretty.

"I'm lookin'," she told the man behind the counter, "for a good friend a mine. Name a Dainty Macklesfield."

The man said, expressionless, "Me, I don't know no one."

"I'd give five quid if someone could tell me where I could find 'im."

"I don't care if you'd give me five feels of your elbow. I don't know the bloke. Don't know no one, me."

"I'm desprit." She turned to Jem. "Do you 'appen to know Dainty Macklesfield, sir?"

"No," Jem said.

"See, I know where I can find 'im an hour from now. 'E's meetin' me in front of the Savoy. But I wants 'im *now*."

"Sorry." Jem put a coin on the counter and rose.

"An hour's time and 'e'll be in front of the Savoy."

Jem walked out. He knew that the place and time was not a message. He knew that he had passed the test if no policemen showed up at the Savoy. He knew his quest was as good as over.

Minerva came back into the living room of her flat from making herself breakfast, a skimped meal of pancakes, cornflakes, three boiled eggs, and toast. She was glad the others had gone. Not that she didn't love them all dearly or that she found their company boring. Nor, absolutely nor, was it that she was at all interested in getting back to page 127 of *Gang-Bang Gal*. Oh, no. She was not in the least keen on finishing that load of filth, though in the name of the cause she supposed she would have to read it eventually. It was simply that she had to write the Chancellor another letter, put on the heat in answer to the latest bland reply to the effect that the Chancellor would not care to buy a raffle ticket on a turkey.

In passing the couch, Minerva put another cushion on the cushion that covered *Gang-Bang Gal.* She sat at her desk and took pen in hand. The opening came easily enough—"My darling angel stallion, my unquenchable beast, my own raging male"—but then she got stuck, wondering how she could improve on the last letter's outpouring of passion.

There was always the book, she told herself brightly and replied to herself harshly that those phrases and words used in the book were unfit even for a swine such as Britain's Chancellor. But they *had* given inspiration before. And they *could* be toned down. And it *was* her duty to make the letters as strong as possible.

She got up, strode to the couch, and circled it with a last-second lurch, flipping an antimacassar onto the two cushions. She would most definitely not read the book. She could find plenty of inspiration in her watercolors.

In a corner Minerva stood before an easel on which rested one of her paintings. She could find in it nothing whatever. She had forgotten what it was supposed to represent. She did, though, rather care for that pillar in pink and mauve which was similar to a . . . a . . .

She went back to her letter. The near-blank page sneered like a blowup of teeth. She toyed with and discarded the idea of writing about the cardigan she was knitting.

Perhaps, she thought, she would find something fairly respectable hidden on page 127 if she read, as she had last night, with her eyes half closed, though sometimes she'd had them fully closed, for sentence after sentence. Those had been terrible sentences, terrible. And wasn't it page 128?

Minerva frowned. Had she forgotten the page number? It was quite feasible. Hadn't she better check to see before she forgot even the approximate number? It would be awful if she had to wade through pages and pages to find her place. Frightful.

She darted to the couch, flung aside antimacassar and cushions, snatched up the book, and opened it at the unusually large bookmark. Yes, the page number was 127. But just to be sure.

Minerva read. Her body tightened from toes to eyelashes. Her heart began to stomp, her face began to heat.

"Yes," she gasped on reaching the bottom of the page. "One twenty-seven is right." With sad hands she closed the book and buried it as before, adding to the pile her bundle of knitting and, as a cooling afterthought, a cloche hat.

She went back to the letter. She couldn't concentrate. She searched for something stirring to think about. The fiasco at Central Exhibition Hall, that's what her mind settled on.

It was sad about Mr. Cease's having to die, but luckily it had been considered an odd accident, and the Group was not involved. Otherwise the venture was a flop. If she had been there on active service, it might have turned out differently. ("Bloomsbury Group Junior was fortunate in that Miss Droplet, the very prominent artist, was in attendance, eschewing the safety of home, where she had earlier decided to stay and read an excellent book.")

Minerva got up firmly, marched to the couch, sat down, and delved freely *Gang-Bang Gal*. She opened it and started to read. She let her body sprawl, her eyelids droop recklessly, and her mouth hang open with voluptuous pleasure. Which state lasted for three pages. Again she found herself growing warm and tense.

She put the book aside and rose. Pacing slowly, nostrils twitching, she admitted to herself that the way she was feeling was not caused by indigestion, as she had formerly insisted, but by an emotion that had, well, a base of naughtiness.

Minerva changed her mind. It was indigestion. Furthermore, if that Mr. Fourpenny came calling with his love-swollen eyes and said wasn't it time they got to know each other better or something like that, she would soon send him packing. She would just like to see him try, that's all.

Minerva's feet almost left the carpet as a knock sounded. Stunned, she walked to and opened the door. There stood

Mr. Fourpenny. He said, "I thought it was time we got to know each other better."

Meltingly, Minerva cooed, "Come *in*."

Downing Street, despite the earliness of the day, looked much the same as usual, with a pair of policemen watching the people who were watching Number 10. Standing on the corner, Jean Quin reflected that it was nice to be back. She had grown fond of the old place. She was even fond of her contacts from Number 11. Green-Jones had sent her roses and a request for a date, Mr. Percival had called to ask if she would care to read some four hundred pages of typescript which would put her in the picture of the Chancellor's life between the ages of twelve and thirteen, and the duplicitous Hobbset she had gotten in touch with to stop his going to a newspaper with Miss Droplet's letters, telling him she had written them herself, admitting that she was the C of E's mistress; since when, Hobbset had telephoned many times to ask couldn't they get together and make a packet out of the story. Jean found the man's purity of corruption rather endearing.

After Jean had been standing on her corner for fifteen minutes, a tall man emerged from Number 11. In morning clothes and Homburg, aged about fifty, hair silver, a monocle glinting in a face like a starving horse, he was one of the most imposing figures Jean had ever seen. No actor could have better overdone the career diplomat.

The man turned onto Whitehall. Trotting to the nearest policeman, Jean performed Avid Provincial Tourist to ask about that man from Number 11 who must be somebody terribly important.

"He is, ma'am," the officer said, giving a sniff which might have been a dash in *Das Kapital*. "He tends the boilers."

"A boilerman?"

"Right. Montague Starchmount. The heart of the establishment."

When the swirl of disappointment and surprise had gone,

Jean thought, Think Assassination. Think exploding boilers.

She hurried away.

Montague Starchmount was striding along at a good clip. Jean followed at a trot, which she had to keep up even when the distance between them had been reduced. She wondered when he was going to take a taxi.

Cabs, however, seemed to hold no interest for Starchmount. He ignored several that were empty. Trotting, panting, Jean began to look progressively less Garbo and more Doormat Meg.

At last they came to a row of shops. Starchmount swung into one. Jean semifell into a doorway and sagged there, waiting. She thought Assassination Starchmount.

In five minutes he reappeared. He came back, retracing his steps. It seemed sure he was returning to Downing Street. Jean told herself she had to act now.

As the man drew level with her doorway she gasped, "Help!"

Starchmount halted. "Did you say something?"

"Help. Please help me."

He removed his monocle, polished it, wound it back, and stared her up and down. "Help you?"

"Yes, please."

"Why on earth should I?"

"I've twisted my ankle," Jean said piteously.

"That is hardly my affair, madam."

Jean agreed that it was not but suggested that it would be terribly charitable of him if he were to call and help her into a cab. He suggested she call one herself. She suggested that a lady should never raise her voice in public.

The starving-horse face twitched with resignation. "Very well," Starchmount said. "One cab." He went to the curb, raised a finger, and brought a taxi to a screeching stop. He came back and helped Jean across with the same finger under her elbow.

By clever maneuvering and sheer body weight, Jean got Starchmount into the cab first. She hurtled out her address and, as they moved off, sat beside her astonished companion, who said, "Look here."

"Terribly kind of you, wanting to help me to my flat. It's not far. I would never have managed without you."

"I see that I have no choice in the matter," he grated. "But do, madam, have the goodness not to lean on me."

Jean slumped back in her corner. She was ready to give up. Without hope, she asked questions. Starchmount told her in snaps his name and that he was a heating engineer and that he thought the weather atrocious.

Because of the stairs, Starchmount used two fingers to support Jean's elbow as they went up to her flat. Inside, he said, "Good day."

Jean pushed him unceremoniously into a chair. "Do smoke a cigarette before you go."

He glared. "I do not smoke."

"Let me fix you a drink."

"I do not partake of alcohol."

Jean let out a growling sigh. She wished she had given him up as useless in the cab. She thought, however, that since she had gotten him this far, she might as well go the whole hog.

"If you'll wait here for just two minutes, Mr. Starchmount, I have something to show you."

"What?"

"You'll see."

"Very well," he said, looking at his watch and rising. "But I shall wait standing up."

Jean went into her bedroom, stripped and put on her robe, came back, and said in an indifferent voice, "I didn't really twist my ankle. The fact is, I had to get to know you. When I saw you striding along Whitehall, something moved inside me. I felt a burst of heat."

"What," he asked, "do you wish to show me?"

"It was love, Mr. Starchmount. I fell in love with you at first sight."

Montague Starchmount took out his monocle, put it away, and produced a folded handkerchief. He sat down. After carefully arranging the crease of his trousers, he opened the handkerchief and spread it across his knees. Then he burst into tears.

In the past hour Sid Fourpenny and Minerva Droplet had progressed to the stage of sitting side by side on the couch. They were both agitated and both driven by determination.

Minerva, hot with altruism, was determined that the love so patently borne her by Mr. Fourpenny should not go unrequited, or even, if it came to that extreme, unconsummated. To aid the timid swain she had drawn the curtains—complaining of the harsh light—and switched on lamps of cozy softness, stacked her record player with soothing music, and served a glass of sherry, medium dry.

Sid was even more self-deluding in his determination to sexually possess the other, although his assumed reason did happen to be gross with truth. Sid would have been astounded at the idea that what started the chain of thought which led to the flat had been Miss Droplet's body in a silky, clinging dress with buttons down the front and bows on the hem. As far as he was concerned, the why of his visit was noble and brilliant, purely of the mind.

Since seeing Minerva being followed from the bookshop by the Socio-Demo-Fascinist, Sid had become convinced that she was an SDF member and spied for them on BGJ. The fact that no SDF's had shown up at CEH had not changed his mind. In fact, as the C of E did not show up himself, it loomed possible that he too was an SDF, for otherwise why should he be trying to ruin the country? It all seemed quite clear to Sid.

He calculated that the best way to deal with an enemy in the camp was not to destroy him but make him into a friend in the camp of the enemy. To this end he would seduce Miss Droplet, turn her into his love slave, and from there into a double agent.

It had taken so long for Sid and Minerva to reach their present stage of intimacy because of fluctuating doubts about willingness to cooperate, Sid's stemming from Minerva's constant movement (she was setting the scene and getting her book hidden) and Minerva's from Sid's movement of equal constancy (he was checking for hidden microphones and cameras).

They continued to dawdle, hardly aware of the nonsense they were mumbling; Minerva had no wish to make the first positive move, and Sid, accepting her as an artist and an idealist, thought the usual approach would be too crude.

"I just adore poetry," Minerva was saying as she throbbed with benevolence.

Sid seized upon his opening. "Love poetry?"

"Oh, yes! I'm sure you write it divinely, Mr. Fourpenny."

"Yes, I'm very good at it."

"Do quote me some," she pleaded.

Sid shook his head, wisely deciding against Eskimo Nell. "I can never remember any when I'm, er, emotionally disturbed."

"Oh, Mr. Fourpenny."

"Ah, Miss Droplet."

The moment, dripping with promise, passed. But they were on the right track. Minerva asked, "Will you read me someone else's love poems? You do read divinely."

Sid assented. He fixed eager eyes on Minerva's swaying roundness as she went to a bookcase and, when she returned to sit a fraction closer, told himself, "She's on, mate."

He took the slim volume. Opening it at random, he began to read. Clear at first, even through the tooth barrier, his words soon became blurred sibilants as he worked at the gradual assault.

Minerva sat as still as a large mouse. She felt Sid's arm go around her waist, felt the hand rise to her shoulder. "Divine words," she murmured, slowly turning her back toward him, being rather taken by a scene on page 98 wherein the heroine is sprawled across the villain's lap.

"My spirit soars aloft," read Sid, wondering what was with the back bit.

("Who knows what passions were released that morning

in flat 2B?") thought Minerva, her body now sideways, her legs on the couch.

"To meet at heaven's portal."

("Miss Droplet, famed artist, was won over by the magic of poetry.") Minerva sank gracefully backward in front of Sid, her arm clumping by his nose.

"While a bunch of the boys were loving it up."

Reaching the end of her descent, Minerva lay supine, head dropped back, eyes closed. She shuddered when Sid's hand came to rest on her stomach.

"If you will open your heart to me," Sid read, game despite the weight on his thighs.

"Divine, divine," she whispered, not meaning the mumbled drone.

Sid, trembling, undid two buttons of the dress.

"Go on!" Minerva gasped. "Er, read on!"

He sneaked his hand inside the dress and caressed her stomach. She whimpered softly. After pausing to jabber off another line, he slid his hand up and met the cynical underband of her brassiere. He tried to probe beneath.

Minerva, her breath making clacking sounds at the back of her stretched throat, performed a mighty rounding of her shoulders. The underband eased. She clacked rapidly as she felt the hand get as far as its knuckles.

". . . *noon* . . . *croon* . . . *loon* . . ." Sid read, his eyes grabbing at words between darts to observe the actions of Minerva, who was now twisting her outer arm behind her back. He felt a hand creep between his legs, and he whinnied.

"Divine," rasped Minerva, struggling with the catch of her bra. "Read on, read on."

With the commotion caused by Minerva's struggle, his own trembling, and the fact that his book hand was entangled with Minerva's free arm, Sid had lost his place. He snatched at phrases in the waving, flapping book.

"See Index!"

"Book Club Edition!"

Minerva tore at the bra catch viciously. ("Miss Droplet, painter of renown, hadn't enough bloody sense to take her rotten bra off beforehand.")

"Copyright reserved!"

With a wrench Minerva broke away the puritanical hooks. She brought back her arm and sagged with a small roar of a sigh.

Sid was highly agitated. His mouth hung open. Sweat gathered between his eyebrows and trickled down his nose. He experienced a violent increase in emotion as he pushed forward the hand that was no longer restrained and felt it cruise between Minerva's breasts.

It cruised between and, sped by overeagerness, swept on until brought to a halt by her throat, at which it fumbled in bewilderment.

"Divine," snapped Minerva. "Go back."

Sid read hoarsely, "Printed in England!"

Minerva gave up all pretense. The time for maidenly modesty had passed. She ripped out Sid's arm, flung herself upright, stood back, and rushingly took off her dress. ("Droplet, the noted painter, stripped off to have a right good bash.")

Sid rose slowly, limply to his feet. He stared in raging delight at the revealed nakedness. His pulses boomed, his head trembled. Minerva reached toward him—and his delight turned to fear. The hands. He had forgotten the hands. He gaped at them as they came graspingly, crushingly closer. His fear and agitation reached a crescendo. He fainted.

The shop of the gunsmith was bare except for a showcase of shotguns behind the counter. Virginius Twyce looked around cheerfully as he entered. He thought it nice for a change to have a task to do that presented no problem, a nice simple innocuous task.

He broke off his hum of pleasure and called in a voice of authority, "Shop!"

The man who slid into position behind the counter was

worn like an old glove salesman, sad of face. "Your pleasure, sir?" he winced.

"I should like," Virginius said airily, "a pistol."

"Beg pardon?"

"A pistol, man. A revolver."

The man became more sad. "Sorry, sir. I can't sell you a handgun."

Virginius leaned forward. "*What* did you say?"

"Terribly sorry."

"You won't sell me a gun?" Virginius was outraged and astonished.

The man backed away. "Can't, sir. It's illegal to sell handguns."

"Illegal! I've never heard of anything so ridiculous in my life. How dare you?"

"It's not me, sir. It's the law."

"The law is a bumbling ass."

"I agree, I agree. It won't let a man turn an honest penny."

"And what about me? How'm I going to get a gun?"

"It's quite a problem, sir, I know."

Virginius glared. "What does *that* mean?"

"Er, it's not easy."

"This is all very sinister and mysterious."

The man had flattened himself against the showcase. "Sorry."

"Are you or are you not going to tell me where I can buy a gun?"

"Well, sir, I know how you might get onto one."

"Might? Might? My good man, you have wasted my coffee break."

"Sorry, sir. I'll give you the address if you want."

Virginius groaned. "Oh, I suppose I can waste my lunch break, too."

"Mind, sir, I don't know this place myself. It's sort of underworld, I reckon. I've been told you can get anything there."

"Very well. Give me your vile address. But this is all most inconvenient. I hope you realize that."

"Yes, sir," the man winced. "Sorry, sir."

Sid Fourpenny came back to consciousness. He found that he was lying in an uncomfortable twist on the couch in Miss Droplet's flat. He remembered. Sitting up, he ran both hands over his face, over skin that was still damp with the clamminess of fear. He thought of those large, plier-strong hands and shuddered anew.

Fully alert now, Sid became aware of Miss Droplet's absence. Hesitantly he called her name. Getting no answer, he searched the flat. No Miss Droplet.

He helped himself to a glass of sherry. He was raising it to his lips when he saw the implication that could be put upon his faint. Minerva might assume that when it came to the crunch, the moment of truth, he was incapable of following through, was not man enough. Sid's mouth dried out at the picture of Miss Droplet telling with giggles of his failure as a man.

He left the sherry and hurried out.

It was quiet now in Jean's living room. The asexual passion of Montague Starchmount, boilerman, was spent. He lolled, dreamy in exhaustion and emotional release, his face looking like that of a horse which is not averse to the odd bit of starvation.

His crying had lasted a long time. It had been done with style and dignity. Leaning forward, he had made well-regulated gurgling noises while letting his tears fall onto the handkerchief. Finally arid, he had given a long sigh and put his handkerchief back in its folds and gratefully accepted a cup of tea.

"Feel better now?" Jean asked, sitting close to him on a stool.

"Thank you, Miss Ninotchka, yes."

"More tea?"

"Thank you, no. I find it too stimulating."

"Perhaps there's something else you'd like," said Jean, who had been moved by the man's weeping.

"Yes. What I would like is to tender to you my sincerest apologies for having given way like that."

"Please don't mention it."

"I must. I must explain." He sat up and screwed into place his monocle. "You see, I broke down because of what you said."

"I understand."

"They were the first kind words I'd been given in years."

"Poor Mr. Starchmount."

He held up a hand. "Please. You'll start me off again."

"Excuse me."

"My late wife treated me harshly, my landlady is a positive ogre, and at my place of employment, well, there has never been a word of thanks or appreciation. My employer simply does not understand me."

"What's he like?"

"A cad."

"Oh?" Jean said brightly.

"A bounder."

"You sound as though you're not fond of him."

"I despise him intensely."

Jean grinned. "A real hatred, in fact."

"A real true genuine hatred, Miss Ninotchka."

"I *knew* you were a man of strong emotions."

"Many is the time I have dreamed of doing something drastic to satisfy my loathing."

"Do tell me," Jean said, hugging herself.

"Well, once I almost turned off the radiators in his bedroom."

"You didn't."

"I did. And it was a particularly cool August. Another time I thought I might write him an anonymous letter, full of abuse, telling him what a rotter he was."

"You're a dangerous man to cross, Mr. Starchmount."

He nodded, looking at his watch. "I must go."

"Oh, no," Jean said, alarmed.

"My boilers, you know."

Jean softened her voice. "Not yet." Moving her robe, she uncovered a good length of thigh.

Montague Starchmount stared rigidly at the wall. "Miss Ninotchka, may I tell you something?"

"Yes, my dear," breathed Jean.

"You won't be offended?"

"I promise."

He closed his eyes while he said, "Your leg is showing."

"Oh."

"Most unseemly. But unseemly of me to notice. I do so hate indelicacy, don't you?"

Covering herself, Jean stated flatly, "I love you, Mr. Starchmount."

"I am going to consider that, Miss Ninotchka, be assured." He rose. "I must go."

"Oh, you can't."

"Yes, yes. Stoking time."

"But you'll come back soon. You must. I can't exist without your presence."

"I know how it is."

"And I want to hear about your work. I'm fascinated. I want you to tell me all about boilers."

Starchmount looked to be on the point of another breakdown. "You are interested?"

"Terribly."

"I *will* come back. Within a few hours. Furthermore I shall give very serious consideration to your offer."

"You're a dear."

He walked to the hall. "It's quite thrilling that you should be interested in boilers. Amazingly enough, few people are. Some are almost the reverse. It's beyond me. There is nothing so magical as being there in a house's very vitals, feeding the friendly monster, tapping its tentacles, watching its dials. The drama of it all. The romance."

"And the danger."

"Yes, indeed, danger too. It's not a career to be gone into lightly. One needs a calling. Unfortunately, my son did not have it, though he tried hard. He gave up, went to the colonies."

"Poor boy."

"Owns a sheep ranch now. It's quite sad."

"Bear up, Mr. Starchmount. Remember my love."

Jean puckered her lips, and Montague asked permission to shake her hand, saying that after all they did know each other quite well now. When he had gone, Jean twirled joyfully, thinking Assassination.

The lady was leaning against a column; creeping up behind her was a man. The lady's face was impassive; the man's was rippling with evil intent. The lady held nothing; the man held a piece of metal with a sharp point.

Closer and closer crept the man, making no sound, picking his way with care. Eyes glinting, he came to within a foot of his goal. He slowly lifted the metal shaft and placed its point a fraction of an inch from the back of the lady's head. His other hand slowly raised a hammer.

"Hey, there!"

Jem Gate lowered his hammer and chisel as he casually looked around. He saw no one to connect with the shout. Looking back at the stone lady, he mused that his idea certainly did have merit. All it needed was the right person faced in the right direction in a suitably deserted place.

"Hey, there!"

This time when Jem turned at the shout, he saw its owner. Making his way through the hunks of masonry was a man in a jacket of chessboard pattern, who had a cheery face and untidy yellow hair. "There you are, then," he said.

"Yes," Jem agreed. "Mr. Macklesfield?"

"Right you are." The man shook Jem's hand with enthusiasm. "But not Dainty. I'm his brother Mel. You're Mr. Gate?"

"Yes."

"I'm very pleased to make your acquaintance."

"Likewise."

"I heard a little rumor from Portuguese Ned that you had a bit of business to throw the way of our Dainty, eh?"

"Yes."

"That's the way, Mr. Gate."

"You telephone?"

"The other night, the Scotland Yard bit? Yes. Checking. We also checked with a contact in your local nick. You're not one of them."

"Girl in café?"

"Me sister. You're clean, Mr. Gate."

"Thank you," Jem said, flattered.

Mel Macklesfield's mouth gave a twist of warning. "I must make it clear that Dainty doesn't do wives or mothers or children under sixteen."

"All right."

"Sentimental, see."

"Commendable."

"Now then, your Intended being okay, would you like to meet our Dainty?"

"Yes, please."

Mel turned his head to the side and called, "Hey, Dai-en-tee!" From the corner of his mouth he said quietly, "He's a bit shy with strangers."

"I see."

"That's why I came along. He's not much of a talker. He needs me to take his part. You could very well talk rings around him, see."

Into view hove a tall man of massive bone structure but little flesh. His clothes hung like split sails from a spar. He had his brother's untidy yellow hair and cheery face, the latter marred by several razor scars. Like a child aware of being watched, he walked loosely and bulged out a cheek with his tongue.

Mel asked, side-mouthed, "Big lad, eh?"

"Doesn't look," Jem said, "vicious."

"Don't you fret. Don't you ever go and fret about our Dainty. Looks mean nothing. When it comes to business, old Daint is the most heartless bastard in the world."

"Good."

Dainty lollingly arrived. He took up a position half to his

brother's rear, made something like a nod in the direction of Jem, and looked at the ground.

Mel rubbed his hands. "Down to the old details, eh? When, where, and who?"

"Tell that later."

Mel nodded. He coughed and said, his mouth sheepish, Dainty the while turning his head away as far as it would go, "Then there's just the little matter of, like, price."

Jem stated, "Hundred pounds."

Mel Macklesfield frowned with his lips. Dainty brought around his head and, before looking at the ground, flashed Jem a look which eloquently backed the claim to his being, in business hours, the world's most heartless bastard.

Jem amended, "Guineas."

Dainty mumbled in his brother's ear. Mel said, "Two hundred."

Jem took a tight grip on his hammer and shook his head. "Too much."

"Not for a perfect, clean job," said Mel. "A Macklesfield job. You're buying the best there is. Ask anyone. I can give you the names of a dozen referees."

"Hundred and ten."

Dainty mumbled, Mel translated. "A hundred and ninety."

"No."

"Mr. Gate, you've got to consider the risk. Our Dainty could go down for a long, long time. Ever so long. He's a man that likes his ale and grub, to mention nothing of the occasional bird. Stir would go very hard with old Daint."

Jem could see that if the bartering went on, its conclusion would be a meeting at a hundred and fifty pounds, which was exorbitant. He decided to make a firm stand.

"Last offer," he said. "One twenty." He stopped Dainty, who was on the way to his brother's ear with a mumble, by adding, "Got no more."

Mel, mouth hurt, asked, "That's your lot?"

"Every penny."

Dainty Macklesfield turned and walked away, swaying,

scuffing his shoes. Mel said, "Wait on, Daint," and to Jem, "I'll see if I can get him to come down a bit."

"One twenty. No more."

Mel's top lip lifted skeptically. "You can do a bit better than six score, Mr. Gate."

"Not a farthing."

"I don't think he'll take it."

"Last offer."

Mel went to where his brother stood scratching moodily at a stone urn. They whispered together. Mel returned with, "Old Daint saw a radio in your office. He's taken a fancy to that radio. He says if you throw it in, you've got a deal."

"Worth twenty," Jem said. "No."

Mel's mouth screwed to the side thoughtfully. "If I can get him to take, say, a hundred and ten plus the radio, are you on?"

"Perhaps."

Mel returned to Dainty, whispered, gestured, came back, and said, "No, he won't take less than a hundred and twenty quid, but he'll tell you what he'll do. If you throw in your radio, he'll give you his transistor set."

Jem was tired of the bargaining. He nodded. "A deal."

Virginius Twyce wore a pained expression as he examined his goal. The address given him by the gunsmith was a curdled-looking bookshop in Soho. However, Virginius mused, if, as the gunsmith had said, the connection was of dubious legality, one could hardly expect a large store on a main road.

He went in. The man serving was plump and bald. Virginius told him, "I want a pistol."

The man laughed. "A pistol? Hotter than a pistol? It's nice to see these old expressions coming back."

"Glad you find humor in my terminology," Virginius said with sour face and tone. "Now perhaps you would like to tell me how much."

"Hold on a bit. What about coloring? Black, brown, blond, and so forth."

"Black."

"There's a little number called Lulu might suit."

"Quick on the trigger?"

"Very. Real hot stuff."

"How much?"

"I'll just make a phone call, see if she's available."

"Who?"

"Lulu."

"Ah, I see. She owns it."

"Owns it!" the man laughed. "I should think she does."

"And she'll have it there with her?"

"You're a card," choked the man.

Virginius frowned. "Stick to business, please. I've got to get back to the office. Will she or will she not have the gun on the premises?"

"Gun?" the man said, becoming wistful. "It's getting very popular this lark with a gun. Never tried it meself."

"Make the telephone call, please."

The man was away for ten minutes. He returned to say, "Lulu hasn't got one. Nor has Shirl. Finally I got onto Pam, and she says okay, she'll have one by the time you get there."

"How much?"

"Twenty quid. But she wants to know what you're going to do with it."

"That," Virginius said coldly, "is none of her business."

"She doesn't want to get hurt, you understand."

Virginius tutted. "It's not going to be used on the lady, so what's the problem?"

"Okay, but how about telling me?"

"Certainly not."

The man brought back his wistful look as he scribbled an address. "Give me a hint, eh?"

"No."

"Would I find it in Kinsey?"

"I think this is a disgrace," Virginius said, taking the card, "drunk in charge of a shop. You should be reported."

"Eh?"

Virginius went outside. He began to hurry. Glancing at his watch, he mused that even the simplest tasks could take an inordinate time. It would be infuriating if he were late back at work.

He found the house, found the right basement door. It was opened to his knock by a girl wearing a dangerously short nightdress. He huffed, "That's another disgrace."

"What is?"

"Your garment."

The girl whined, "It's too cold to stand around naked."

"Are you drunk as well?"

"Am I who?"

"Never mind. Where's the gun?"

She produced it from behind her back. "Come inside."

"No time." He thrust money at her, took the gun, and turned. "Good day."

"Where you goin'?" she yelped.

"To the office, of course," he called back. "And that's none of your business, either."

Lady Severn had thought Assassination so long and so thoroughly that her insteps had started to ache. She had come up with nothing definite. In fact, she herself would be the first to admit that none of her schemes was particularly striking. The most attractive was the lifting of the Chancellor from outside his house by means of a hook attached to a wire lowered from a helicopter, taking him to a great height, and letting him fall to his death on the roof of the Palladium. The other schemes were inclined to be fanciful.

Madge was glad when lunchtime came and she was able to think Two Poached Eggs. She had just finished eating as the bell rang. She opened the door to a perspiring, breathless Minerva Droplet, who thumped in without a word and began to pace the living room.

Madge returned to her seat. "I know how it is, dear. I've thought and thought."

"Yes," Minerva said without elaborating, without mentioning that her thinking and thinking had not been on ways and means connected with the Chancellor's death.

When Sid Fourpenny had fallen unconscious, Minerva, giving fierce grunts of rage and frustration, had flung on her clothes and left. She had not stopped walking since, even though her fury had abated under the onslaught of reason. She was propelled now by excitement.

Reason, Droplet-style, now made her say, "Lady Severn, I have to tell you something which may be painful." ("Minerva, painter par excellence, was not one to flinch from the truth.")

"Oh, dear."

"About Mr. Fourpenny. He came to see me this morning, and it was soon clear that behind his visit there was a motive sinister and terrible."

"Our poet?"

"Our poet," Minerva said, still pacing. "A fine poet he may be, but he is also a sex maniac."

Madge was startled. "Think what you are saying, my dear."

"I am. Believe me, I am. I don't make these accusations lightly."

"I'm sure you are mistaken."

"I'm not. And there's worse to come. Mr. Fourpenny is not merely a sex maniac. He is one who, if he can't have his lecherous way with his victims, *kills them.*"

"Miss Droplet!" Lady Severn gasped.

"I know, I know, it's a shock. It was a shock to me when I found out."

"How? When?"

"This morning. At my flat an hour or so ago."

"He told you all this?"

Minerva shook her head as she strode out dramatically. She was having a marvelous time. "He tried it on me."

"I cannot believe it."

"Listen. I've turned him down so often, spurned his advances so firmly, that he came along today with one thing in his mind—my death. First of all, of course, he tried once more to possess me, but I resisted."

"Er, why?"

Unhearing, Minerva plunged on, "The same thing, obviously, happened with Pat Single. Mad with desire for me, he went to her. She, too, for some odd reason, turned him down. He killed her in the way she described when she spoke to us from beyond the grave."

"She didn't mention sex. And anyway, that Machiavelli . . ."

"He came close to success with me. Homicidal success. At one point he actually had his hand on my throat. I was too clever for him. I pulled it away. Then even more cleverly, though I say it myself, I stunned him into momentary pause by disrobing. Yes, I took off all my clothes."

"Good for you."

"The ruse worked better than expected. Instead of merely pausing in his attack, he fainted. Stricken, no doubt, with remorse on seeing the beauty of my body."

"No doubt."

"I was able to put on my clothes and make good my escape. Since then I have walked and walked, wrestling with my conscience. And I have an idea I was followed." Stalking to the window, she looked out.

"If he's there," Lady Severn said, "tell him to come in."

Minerva turned. "What!"

"I'll leave you two alone together. Let you work out this wee lovers' tiff."

"Lady Severn," Minerva said severely, "everything I have told you is gospel. He did try to kill me. He did kill Miss Single. Something's got to be done. That's why I've been wrestling with my conscience."

Madge frowned. "What do you propose?"

"I shall have to go to the authorities."

"Oh, really now, my dear. It's not as serious as all that. After all, it was a personal thing, nothing to do with the Group."

"It makes no difference."

"But, my dear, if you go to the police, the Group will be implicated. We cannot have that."

"It will be difficult, I realize. Still, I can't allow a sex maniac to go marauding through the streets, attacking beautiful young girls."

"All right, be a spoilsport if you will, but wait until after our mission is accomplished."

Minerva ignored her hostess, because Minerva had not the slightest intention of going to the authorities. She was going for a walk to put another, more useful-for-future-use slant on Sid's faint and aims. But she had no wish to be cheated out of her moment of drama.

She stalked to the door. ("Miss Droplet, artist of international fame, made a noble figure that day as she reached her momentous decision.")

Lady Severn said, "Wait!"

"My mind is made up!" Minerva cried, and, hoping she was right about having been followed, rushed out.

"Help!" wailed Lady Severn, running to the telephone. "Help!"

Minerva came out into the street. She looked right, left, right again. She saw no face she knew. Perhaps he was being clever about it, she thought.

She began to walk, swaying her hips. She told herself she had been foolish in the extreme to rush out of her flat like that when dear Sid fainted, since it was now perfectly obvious and logical that his faint had been on account of seeing her body in all its natural glory: a swoon of ecstasy, coupled with the explosion of hope, the poor darling having been fretting and praying for months for even a touch of her hand, a glimpse of her unclothed arm, a smile of more than friendly warmth. It was cruel of her to have tortured him so in the past.

Minerva came to the corner and looked around again. Still no familiar face. She dawdled for a while before crossing to the other side and continuing her leisurely walk.

Yes, she thought, Sid Fourpenny (such a sweet name) was

a virgin, one of nature's innocents. Never in his poetic life had he indulged in the carnal, saving himself for that which conquers all. No wonder the blood had charged to his head and rendered him unconscious when, after years of dreaming of beauty, he had at last actually seen it in the flesh.

Innocence, of course, lack of experience, accounted for all his hesitancy and fumbling. That sweet amateurish way he had caressed her stomach, her naked stomach, and had then expected her bra to magically remove itself. The way his hand had slid between her naked breasts. An expert would have seized them and felt their firm roundness, their silky surface, their . . .

Minerva touched the center of her top lip with her tongue thinking of a scene which had begun in similar style in *Gang-Bang Gal.* She continued to think of the scene, losing herself in it, until a minor collision with another pedestrian brought her back from the book and made her realize how erratic had been her course.

She set herself straight, fingering the perspiration off her brow.

She noticed that she was passing a police station. She kept passing. It had been, she admitted, naughty of her to exaggerate that teeny bit to Lady Severn by accusing Sid of murdering Miss Single out of thwarted passion. Poor Pat had not been capable of rousing passion in a blind tent pole. Sid had never given her a first glance, and had she been standing sideways, he wouldn't have seen her anyway. Of course he hadn't killed her, she had killed herself out of remorse for stabbing Tony Zero, although she might have just been saying that, in the suicide note, not wanting it known even after death that she was rusted with envy of her divinely endowed colleague and had finally given up the hope of achieving such proportions.

Minerva sighed at the danger to others in one's being, as she believed it was called, stacked. Like the heroine in that vile loveless book. For her beauty she had been cut dead in the street on page 63. Then on page 72. Yes, that was a terrible page.

Minerva lived through the terrible page, turned over and lived through the next. Her pulse quickened, her brow produced sweat, her direction wavered.

She was brought cruelly from page 81 by another jostling. She stopped, murmuring an apology in exchange for the snarl from the jostled. She saw that she was in the West End, the roadway thick with traffic, the pavement aswarm with people. Turning, she searched the crowd.

Isn't that—she thought of a figure that moved into a doorway—no, maybe not.

It occurred to her that as nothing had happened, it was possible she had not been followed after all. So she might as well go home. In fact, that was very likely where she would find the heartsick poet, still waiting, endlessly faithful. And there was that loathsome book to finish.

Minerva moved to the curb in search of a taxi. Around her the crowd moved closely. An engaged cab went by, a bus approached. She felt a firm shove in her back. She tried to twist around to protest, but she was already falling—and the bus was coming. "Sid!" she screamed.

five

The Cause had been presented with its best bet thus far. The Chancellor of the Exchequer was to attend a rally-fete the next morning, behind a public house in Kent, where there would be fine opportunities for assassination; two days later he was scheduled to leave on an extended tour of Swiss banks. The Group had preparations to make.

The news of the Chancellor's imminent availability and absence was in the evening newspapers' young afternoon editions. Jean Quin saw the item and telephoned Lady Severn.

"How marvelous, Jean, dear."

"Yes, I think this is it. Our big chance. We've got to give it all we've got."

"We must lay careful plans."

Jean asked, "Have you thought of a good method yet?"

"No, have you?"

"Not a thing. Perhaps our male members will produce the ideas."

"Let us pray so."

"In any case, a rehearsal, that's what we need. Full dress."

Lady Severn said she would consider the matter and call back. Hardly had she put down the receiver than she was summoned to lift it again. She heard Sid Fourpenny say, "I have bad news for you."

"About the C of E?"

"No, Miss Droplet."

"What?"

"Minerva Droplet, paintings and that."

"What about Minerva?"

"She's dead."

Lady Severn glared into the mouthpiece. She wet her lips thoroughly before asking, "Did I hear you right?"

"Yes."

"But she left here no more than half an hour ago, alive and well, if somewhat distraught. She can't be dead."

"Well, she is."

"This is terrible, terrible," Madge said, tears underlining her eyes. "I cannot believe it."

"I saw the body. I helped some other men lift it onto a stretcher."

Lady Severn shook her head sadly. "What happened?"

"I was walking in the West End, see, when I heard passersby talking about the accident up ahead. I went on and saw that the victim was our Miss Droplet. It seems she'd walked right in front of a bus."

"How terrible," moaned Lady Severn.

"And mysterious," said Sid Fourpenny.

"Eh?"

"I have not yet finished my investigations, but soon I might have something real funny to report. Curious like."

Madge put a hand to her brow. Things were becoming far too complicated. First Minerva Droplet comes and rampages around the room spouting strange and evil accusations about sex and murder, next she falls under a bus and gets herself killed, and now the putative sex/homicidal maniac (what drivel) himself is talking about secret investigations. Far too complicated.

"You still there?" Sid Fourpenny asked.

"Yes," she said. Keeping to the simple and known, she set the mourning period at three hours and a time, 6 P.M., for the assassination rehearsal and asked Mr. Fourpenny to apprise the others of these. Ringing off, she indulged in a prolonged bout of weeping before dressing herself completely in black and sitting on a hard chair as far from the fire's comfort as she could get.

Sid had found the address without trouble: He looked in a telephone directory under Socio-Demo-Fascinist. He was on his way to their headquarters, on his motor-assisted bicycle, having decided that under the circumstances it would be stupid to obey the call for three hours of mourning.

He was greatly disturbed about Miss Droplet. Had he been wrong about her spying on the Group, about her being an SDF? Perhaps she had been spying *on* the SDF's to find out what they were learning in their spying on the Chancellor, if, that is, he was not an SDF himself, in which case she could have been spying to find out why he wasn't. . . .

Sid's thinking faltered. He coughed and took another abstract direction. What if Minerva *had* been a member of the Socio-Demo-Fascinists, with a task that was now completed—that of getting one of the Group in SDF power, and that one being Sid Fourpenny. Now, it was quite possible that he had not fainted at the Droplet's, that he had been given a whiff of gas or a drug (the sherry, mm?) or had been hypnotized; that once unconscious he had been photographed in a compromising situation (that bookshop and its photos, eh?), that the enemy's next step would be to approach him with their evil evidence and try a spot of blackmail.

Yes, Sid thought, revving toughly, it was quite possible. And if it were so, they'd picked on the wrong boy. No one could pull a fast one on Mrs. Fourpenny's lad and get away with it. He'd soon show the Socio-bloody-Demo-sodding-Fascinist bastards a thing or two, and no mistake.

Leaning grimly forward over the handlebars, swerving around corners at a manic twenty miles an hour, Sid covered the last stretch to the home of the SDF, a broken-down ex-shop on a wide commercial road south of the river. The window contained a large poster of an outpointing finger with the slogan "YOUR COUNTRY DOESN'T NEED A GOVERNMENT."

Sid parked his bicycle untidily and strode into the shop. Inside were some chairs, a table, and one man. Conveniently, it was the man who had followed Minerva Droplet from the bookstore, the man who had made a complaint in Hyde Park. He was back in uniform now.

Sid folded his arms aggressively. "What's all this?"

The man stopped sorting a pile of pamphlets. "It's the headquarters of—"

"I know that," Sid snapped, teeth ungritted. "Don't try to be funny."

"The SDF is never funny. Humor is the poison of the entertaining minority bloodsuckers."

"That's as may be. What I want to know is, what about photographs?"

"You've got the wrong place."

"Look, what about Miss Droplet?"

The man stared. "You know her—Miss Droplet?"

"I *did.*"

"Finished? Well, it was nothing to do with me."

"Oh, no?"

"No. If you saw me following her about a time or two, it was not because I was interested, shall we say, romantically. Not my type."

Sid unfolded his arms in puzzlement. "Not your type?"

"No. I was following her to find an opportunity to give her a good bashing, if you'll excuse the crude expression. I wanted to get my own back for the way she showed me up in Hyde Park."

"Yes, I was there."

The man nodded. "Thought you looked familiar. Anyway, I didn't bother finally. I was giving too much weight away."

"Big one," Sid agreed sympathetically.

"Therefore, if you had the impression that I had anything to do with her being finished with you, please discard same. My interest was purely malicious."

Sid said, "Well, you'll be surprised to know that she's dead. She fell under a bus."

"Really?" smiled the man. "What a shame."

"I'm in mourning," Sid said loftily.

"Sorry, old man. It's annoying to lose a loved one."

"Minerva Droplet was a star member of Bloomsbury Group Junior."

"Yes," the man said thoughtfully, "yes. That group. Look here, why don't you sit down and tell me all about it?"

"I should think not," snubbed Sid.

"Very well. Sit down, and I'll tell you all about the Socio-Demo-Fascinists."

"Oh, all right."

Montague Starchmount, heating engineer, sat restfully alone in the living room of Mrs. Jean Quin's apartment. He was preparing word for word what he would say when Miss Ninotchka came out of her bedroom, to where she had gone an hour before after admitting him to the flat, saying she was in mourning for a friend and couldn't see him for a while yet. Montague Starchmount had been content to wait, practicing, polishing his monocle, for he was in no hurry, and he found Miss Ninotchka's behavior admirable.

Jean, in the bedroom, glanced at her watch. She was relieved to see that more than half the mourning period was over, which would suffice. One needn't be too exact about these niceties.

Rising from the bed, she bathed her tear-reddened eyes and began to get ready for her guest, which meant subduing her hair, scouring her face free of cosmetics, and dressing in her most demure high-necked suit, thickest stockings, and flattest shoes.

The preparation was worthwhile. When she entered the living room, Mr. Starchmount rose with a gratified smile on his starving-horse face.

"You look beautiful, my dear," he murmured, bowing over her hand and almost touching it with his lips.

"Thank you, Mr. Starchmount."

Jean sat on a straight chair; her guest returned to the couch. He said, after arranging the crease of his trousers,

"Miss Ninotchka, since our last meeting, this morning, which was also our first meeting—can that be so?"

"It is so. Curious and wonderful, is it not?"

"Indeed. Quite wonderful, because since that meeting, my life has undergone a considerable change."

Jean lowered her eyes. "Yes?"

"Yes. You see, I have given you and your protestations of love my deepest cogitation, just as I promised."

"That was thoughtful of you, Mr. Starchmount."

"Not at all. It behooved me. But to proceed. In this short time, taking into account your devotion to me, your natural charm, and obvious breeding, your burning interest in boilers, I have come to form a strong attachment for you."

Jean gave a well-bred sigh.

"In short," went on the heating engineer, "I would like you to know that I reciprocate, though no doubt to a lesser degree. In time, however, I believe that your love will be fully requited."

Jean again lowered her eyes. "Mr. Starchmount, I hardly know what to say."

"Perhaps, if I may make so bold, it might be rather jolly if you called me by a less formal name. Leave off the Mr. Just call me Starchmount."

"Thank you—Starchmount."

"Now, the next step is, I wish to prove my good faith. I wish to show you that I am genuine in my feelings, that I am not simply taking advantage of your declaration to foist myself upon you. I want to prove my devotion."

"I see."

"Perhaps you can make a suggestion. Is there a deed I can do to prove myself worthy and true?"

"What, for instance?"

"That I leave entirely to you."

"Well," Jean said hesitantly, "there is something, yes, but I fear 'tis somewhat of a mammoth."

"Name it."

Jean could hardly believe that this was happening. It was almost as if the boilerman knew what she wanted, knew the aims of Bloomsbury Group Junior, and was offering himself as a solution.

Hiding her excitement she said, "Anything?"

"Yes. There could be nothing too great."

"There must be some deeds that would be."

Starchmount shook his head firmly. "You have shown me a kindness and an interest that I have never known before."

"Well, listen, your boilers, are they in good condition?"

"Marvelous condition."

"Mm."

"The rosiest of pink, thanks to me."

"Yes, but supposing, just supposing, that one day your boilers were to explode."

Starchmount stared. His face paled to palomino. His monocle fell. One hand started to twitch.

Realizing that she had gone too far but also that by doing so she had helped herself—that death by comparison was notably mild—Jean said, "It doesn't bear thinking about, does it? And naturally it could never happen, as the boilers are in the capable hands of your good self."

Starchmount began calming and retrieved his monocle. "This has nothing to do with . . ."

"No no, I was getting off the track."

"The deed, please."

Bracing herself, Jean blurted, "I'd like you to kill someone for me."

"I see," Starchmount said, continuing to calm.

Jean relaxed. "That wouldn't be asking, er, too much?"

"Mmm, I don't think so, no."

She was smitten by an idea of genius. She said, "The person is the one responsible for my friend's death, the friend I am mourning."

"The villain."

"Yes, he is a villain. A rotter and a cad."

"What did he do?"

Jean looked aside. "There are some things, Starchmount, that a lady cannot mention."

"Quite," he said happily. "Do forgive me for asking."

"You're forgiven."

"Thank you. And you wish to see this vile person dead?"

"Yes. It would be useful if you could do the killing tomorrow morning, around eleven. Could you get time off?"

"I believe it could be arranged."

"Wonderful. It's in Kent. I'll meet you there and give you a gun, and you just do it."

"Righto. Who is the bounder, by the by?"

Jean braced herself again. "Someone you know."

"Really?"

"It's the Chancellor of the Exchequer."

Starchmount's horse features were shifted by a thin, thin smile. "In that case, I should be delighted."

The Socio-Demo-Fascinist officer, whose name was Commander Salem, had been talking for a long time. He talked well. His voice had the sweet, soothing, doubt-lulling qualities of a confidence-trickster's or a successful dentist's. His treatment of abstracts made the commonplace seem startling and the trite a revelation, made the unorthodox sound conservative and the blasphemous holy. He would have excellently served, rising to the level of caviar and ulcers, as a used-car salesman.

Sid Fourpenny sat in a daze, his blurred eyes fixed on Commander Salem's face—which with changes of great gentleness produced smiles, pouts, and sad frowns—while his wondering ears tuned to the caressing voice. Sid was filled with peace and longing.

Commander Salem at last leaned back. "Are you at one with me?"

"Yes," Sid mumbled, blinking himself alert and drawing in air through his nose. "Yes, I am."

The officer reached on the table to get a form and a pen, which he set down in front of Sid. "Put your signature on the dotted line, cousin."

Sid signed the paper. His hand was vigorously shaken by Commander Salem, who said, "Congratulations. You are now a member of the Socio-Demo-Fascinist League."

"Thank you," Sid said, and added shyly, trying out the new form of address, "cousin." He found it to his liking. The term had warmth and a reek of good-fellowship. He felt suddenly proud to belong to this organization of breadth and stature. It was not merely a small crew of people piddling around in Bloomsbury; it was a vast network covering all Greater London with thousands of members in two or three districts.

"Your aims will have to be higher now," the Commander said.

"That's it," Sid muttered. He thought soulfully of giving himself up to SDF aims, which aims themselves he seemed to have forgotten.

"You've made a very wise decision."

"Thanks." His mind on the point that had sent him into his initial daze and rendered everything else the officer had said unintelligible, Sid asked, "And, er, the birds?"

"Pardon me?"

"You know, the girl members."

"You'll meet them soon. We have hundreds. Aged from eighteen upward."

"Yes, yes."

"They're all beautiful, all freethinkers."

Sid gritted his teeth hotly.

Commander Salem walked him to the door. "Don't forget, cousin. I want a complete report on the doings of the gang which you cleverly joined before approaching us for membership."

"Check."

"And any that you can swing over to us will be greatly appreciated."

Sid nodded, lifted his eyebrows, smiled. The other's words had brought into focus a way for him to get somewhere with Mrs. Jean Quin. All he had to do was let her know of his new affiliation. She would then, most certainly, go to work on him as she had been doing with the staff of Number 11. He would waver endlessly, necessitating seduction after seduction.

Sid was still smiling when the commander, after shaking his hand again outside, said, "That man over there, he gave us a funny look. Do you know him?"

Sid's face solemned as he looked across the street at the retreating form of Virginius Twyce.

Virginius hailed a taxi. It stopped, he got in, it sped away. He had decided to try another area. Even over here south of the river the florist's shops looked equally formidable. It had been a traumatic enough experience going to the boss and asking for the rest of the afternoon off, complaining of a headache, but following through with his idea of buying a wreath for Tony Zero, who was being buried today, was proving much more frightening.

Virginius could just imagine the reaction if he were to go into a florist's and state his need.

The woman's face twists with dismay. "Maybe—maybe I didn't hear you right."

"Well, I really don't know."

Her hand stretches toward a pair of scissors, finds the distance too great, comes back to clasp the other at her chest. "My hearing has been a bit off lately."

Virginius repeats his requirement.

The woman shudders. "A *wreath?*"

"A small one."

"A wreath, though."

"Well, if it's not too much trouble."

"But they're for *dead* people."

"Er, yes."

"People in coffins," she says, glancing around fearfully. "I dare say."

Her hands clasp each other tighter and press closer to her bosom. "People who've *died.*"

"A very, very small one, actually. Minute."

"What a horrid, sinister thing to want. I've never heard the like."

Virginius bites into his bottom lip. "A dinky little thing."

"A *wreath!*"

"Perhaps just a bunch of flowers."

Her voice rises. "Why come to me?"

"Just a couple of old flowers," Virginius says, trembling, looking behind him at the door, where people are gathering, staring in.

"Why come to me with your sinister requests for things for the dead?"

"A joke. It's a joke. No one's dead. I really want some roses."

"Her voice rises to a shriek as the door bursts open. *"Roses?"*

Virginius faded out the terrible scene by pulling down brutally one of the folding seats. He changed places and thought, No, the idea was nice, but he would have to give it up. Tony Zero could do without the token of respect. It might take all day to find a small florist's run by an old, feeble lady who was simpleminded.

He stopped the cab, paid it off. He would go on foot the rest of the way to Bloomsbury, fill in the time until six.

As he walked, he wondered what he could say at the rehearsal. Although he had thought Assassination madly, he still had come up with nothing. It was a foolish daydream, the picture he had formed of the Chancellor stabbed, put in a cardboard box, which was secured with chains and locks, covered with flowers, hung from a rafter, and finally thrown in front of an electric bus.

Which reminded Virginius of Minerva Droplet. The whole thing was a shock to the system. Another true artist gone, bewildered by thoughts of sex.

Which reminded Virginius of Sid Fourpenny. It occurred to him how odd it was to have seen the poet being cozy with the Socio-Demo-Fascinists. It seemed quite out of character. Dreamers didn't mix with men of action. He wondered if he should tell the others and concluded not. It was a small matter.

Virginius returned his thoughts to the rehearsal. Even though he had no solution to offer, no super scheme for doing away with the Beast of Downing Street, he had, after all, managed to get hold of a gun. That should excuse him a little when he failed to match the ruses which his brilliant friends would doubtless put forward. The gun was loaded moreover, which made it much more useful.

Proud of his success, Virginius was tempted to bring out the weapon and toy with it casually as he walked. He desisted, because those who saw him would know he was showing off and would be embarrassed, and he would then be embarrassed for their embarrassment, knowing very well that he wasn't showing off.

The end of the period of mourning being respectably long past, Jem Gate thought it time he tidied up his bit of business. He left the sculpture he was working on for Relentable Cease and went into his office. Lifting the telephone receiver, he dialed the number given him by the Macklesfields. The answering voice he recognized as belonging to brother Mel.

"Gate here."

"Hello there, Mr. Gate," Mel said breezily. "Everything okay?"

"Fine."

"That's good. Any development?"

"Yes," Jem said. "Time set."

"The time for the dispatching of your Intended?"

"Right."

"Goodo. It comes at just the right moment. Details, please."

After being told time and place, Mel asked, "And the Intended?"

"Tell at scene."

"You'll be there, Mr. Gate?"

"Yes."

"Fair enough," Mel said. "In fact couldn't be better. There'd be no mistakes that way."

"True."

"Now. About payment."

"Afterward."

"Yes, but look, our Dainty's got to pay an installment on his television set first thing in the morning. That's why I said you called at the right moment, see."

"See."

"You couldn't give him the lolly early on, could you?"

Jem, who was no fool, said, "No."

Mel clicked his tongue. "Oh, well. Can't be helped. Payment afterward at your place, eh?"

"Right."

"Okay. And don't worry, Mr. Gate. Old Daint, he'll be there on time. With a Macklesfield job, you can be sure. Ta-ta."

Lady Severn had changed from weeds back to her tweed suit and had a cheerful fire going by the time the first of the Group arrived at six for a rehearsal of the Chancellor's end. Nevertheless, she and Mrs. Quin took the opportunity of female aloneness to have a quiet weep over the death of Minerva Droplet, though each was in truth moved less by the bereavement than by seeing how moved was the other. So much so, in Jean Quin's case, that she was tempted to cheer Lady Severn up by telling her of the arrangement with Montague Starchmount. Being a down-to-earth person, however, caution prevailed. She knew there was no reason to suppose that tomorrow's adventure would meet with any more success than had any of the others. Starchmount would fill the breach. The show would go on. She would be the hit of the Group, the first heroine of the Cause.

The second to arrive, heralded by the put-put of his motor-assisted bicycle, was Sid Fourpenny. He entered at speed, looking unruffled.

Sid had spent an anxious, haste-wracked time since seeing Mr. Twyce near the headquarters of the SDF. First he had caught up with Twyce's cab, lost it again in traffic, then caught up once more only to find the cab empty. After that he had sped through the streets searching. No Virginius Twyce. Last, coming aware of the time, he had hurtled on to get to Bloomsbury first.

Straightening his tie and hair, he asked, "Er-um-er-um, no one else here yet?"

"No."

"Not Mr. Twyce even?"

"No."

"Did he phone to say, um, eh?"

"There is no reason why anyone should telephone," Lady Severn said. "Do sit down and recover from driving that dreadful machine of yours."

Sid perched on the edge of a chair. Twyce, he thought, had not yet talked. The thing to do now was stop him before he could, even if he wasn't going to, if possible.

Sid sat on tension-hard buttocks, chatting jerkily to Mrs. Quin, hardly aware of what he said, until finally, after Mr. Gate's arrival, in came Virginius Twyce, who ventured no word nor sign out of the ordinary, greeting everyone, including Sid himself, as nervously normal. Sid relaxed to watchfulness.

After some talk in subdued voices of Miss Droplet, their loss, her shocking death, Lady Severn asked the poet if he had composed a few lines for the occasion. The poet admitted that he had not.

"Very well," the hostess said briskly. "Let us get down to business. First, have we managed to get a weapon, Mr. Twyce?"

Virginius, swaying with modesty, put the revolver on the table. Everyone examined it with interest. "Careful," Virginius warned, "it's loaded."

Lady Severn rubbed her hands. "The next thing is, who knows anything about this place in Kent?"

Jean Quin: "I've been there two or three times. They hold all kinds of dos there. I'll describe it."

The rally, it seemed, would be held in a one-acre meadow. There would be all the fun of the fair: swings for those wanting to gain height, roundabouts for those wanting to pretend they were getting somewhere; coconut stalls for those too shy to throw in the real world, small cars for those whose oblique aim on the roads was to dodge; simple ball games for the strong, ghost house for the weak, moon rocket for those too old to ever see it happen; hall of mirrors for the very married, dark maze for the unlikely to be; helter-skelter for the failed teasers and voyeurs. In the center of the attractions and the refreshment tents would be a table attended by party officials and, at the right moment, the Chancellor of the Exchequer, who would make a speech to which no one would listen except said party officials.

"If you've seen one of these things," Jean finished, "you've seen 'em all."

Lady Severn asked, "How about the table?"

The long table would be covered with Commonwealth flags. The officials stood on one side; on the other side lay an open space in which the eager masses could gather.

"How about policemen?"

"I've never seen any there. Not in the center. I dare say they're kept away in case they'd spoil the friendly, family atmosphere."

"Anyway," Virginius said, "this is strictly party. No hecklers, no trouble."

Lady Severn gave herself a hug. "It sounds perfect. There's nothing to stop us. We can plan anything we like."

"I think," Virginius said, "we should make the plan as simple as possible. In other words, why don't we just march up to the table, point the gun, and fire?"

Lady Severn complained about the presence of the officials. "They might be as thick as flies around the C of E."

Jem Gate suggested, "Diversion."

"Of course. Draw them away. And I've got the perfect idea. I'll faint near one end of the table, and Mrs. Quin will faint near the other. The officials will come running."

"Won't the Chancellor come running as well?" asked Jean.

"That rotter? Certainly not. He wouldn't dream of such a thing."

"That's all well and good," Virginius said, "but we still have to think of the getaway."

Reluctantly Lady Severn agreed. "Yes, I suppose we do."

"Even without policemen there'll still be plenty of people around to pounce on us."

"Let us put our thinking caps on. All think Getaway."

The five remaining members of Bloomsbury Group Junior began to think. They circled the room, heads down, wandering in and out of the furniture. Mrs. Quin, who had everything arranged, thought of the present given her by Montague Starchmount, a hand-drawn plan of Number 11's boiler room. Jem Gate, who also had everything arranged, nevertheless thought Getaway because he wouldn't want to go against Lady Severn's wishes. Virginius Twyce thought, with a twang of nerves, of having to rush through crowds and bump into people boorishly and not be able to stop to apologize. Madge Severn thought Dramatic Faint.

Sid Fourpenny thought what he had been thinking all the while the others had talked: kill, kill, kill. He had so far failed in his search for a solution. Trouble was, he mused, he had never been able to kill anything, not even an ant.

He got an idea. It was so marvelous that he laughed.

Jean Quin turned to him from the table. "Did you say something?"

"No—yes. Yes, I did. Listen, everybody. I've got it. There's no need for us to take risks. We'll let the Chancellor kill *himself*."

"Don't follow," Jem said.

"Listen. One of us, disguised as a press photographer, goes to the table, hands the C of E the gun, and asks him to pose with it pointing to his head. A gag picture. We say, of course, that the gun's a toy and ask him to pull the trigger."

Sid looked around. "How does it sound?" he asked, thinking himself that it sounded ridiculous.

The others seemed to think the same. Virginius Twyce asked, "Why should he pull the trigger?"

"If he thinks it's only a toy, why shouldn't he?" Sid pressed his strongest point. "The Chancellor won't be able to resist —you know how he loves publicity."

"We could still do our fainting act," Madge Severn murmured.

Hotly Sid persuaded, "Let's try it out, see how it feels. Let's practice it. I'll be the photographer."

Jean Quin said, "I'll be the Chancellor."

"But you're not a man," Sid objected. "Mr. Twyce would be better."

"But I can act."

"We'll take turns," Lady Severn said. "And as I was the one who thought it all up, this fainting thing, I claim first go."

"Agreed," said Jem Gate.

"Very well," Sid Fourpenny said, speaking through his teeth for more than one reason. "We'll take turns."

Jem strode to the table. "Check safety." He turned and handed the revolver to Lady Severn, who held it in both hands as though it were an egg.

Virginius Twyce held up a finger. "Wait a minute. True enough, to get the right feeling it should be a man. Let me."

Grudgingly Lady Severn handed him the gun.

"That's right, that's right," Sid said, sweating well. "Now give it to me, and I'll hand it to you and ask you to pose, see."

Virginius gave the gun to Sid. "How exactly shall I do it?"

"Just put it to your temple."

"But how? I've never done anything like this before."

Sid placed the nose of the gun to the side of his head. "That way. Then, when I tell you, pull the trigger. Like this."

The noise of the shot was monstrously loud. Everyone froze with faces stretched wide, except Sid Fourpenny, who crashed to the floor and lay still, his temple a red mess.

Virginius became mobile first. In the heavy silence he knelt down and leaned over the fallen. Lady Severn, holding her throat, asked, "Is he . . . Is he . . ."

Virginius looked around at her, puzzled. "Is he *what?*"

"Well, you know, dead."

"Oh, yes."

Madge burst into tears. Jean Quin collapsed in a chair. Jem Gate wrung his hands.

Virginius took the cloth off the table and covered the body, went out of the flat, and said in a loud voice, "Sorry, Lady Severn, that was foolish of me to let off a firework." He came in again.

"Positive," Jem was saying, "catch was on. All my fault."

"No, no," Lady Severn sobbed, "don't blame yourself. Accidents will happen."

Jean sighed. "Poor Mr. Fourpenny. He worked so hard."

"You know," Virginius said worriedly, "I saw him today with an SDF man, and it's just occurred to me that he might have been doing undercover work for the Cause. And now it's all come to nothing."

The others groaned.

Controlling her sobs, Lady Severn said, "There will be a ten-minute period of mourning. Excuse me." She went through to her bedroom, put on her black hat, and sat down. The tears flowed afresh.

Five gone, she thought, rocking in her sorrow. Five dear, devoted friends. Each cut off tragically in his or her prime. And not one of them had ever caused her a moment's sadness, good children all. That was something. But who would be next?

Jem Gate, grave of face, looked at the mantel clock. "Time's up."

Jean Quin turned from the window, Virginius came out of the corner in which he had been sitting, and Lady Severn reappeared, hatless, dabbing her eyes. She asked, "Now what?"

"Well," Jean said, "there's no one to whistle our unfinished anthem, and no one to recite a poem."

"I meant, dear, what are we going to do about Mr. Fourpenny?"

Virginius said, "We've got to get rid of the body."

"We?" asked Jem.

"This accident can't very well be reported, can it?"

"Suppose not."

"Not if we want to keep out of it ourselves."

"And we've got to do that," Madge Severn said. "We'd better get rid of the body."

Jem nodded. "Second that."

"Look," Jean said, "as he did, after all, really shoot himself, let's take him home. It'll be assumed that he committed suicide on account of his business was failing."

Madge asked, "Was it?"

"No."

"Then that's out. In any case, we would have to leave the gun, too, and we need it."

"Next of kin?" Jem mused aloud.

Jean shook her head with Bette Davis vigor. "I don't think he had any. I do know he lived alone."

"The body," Virginius said firmly. "Let's concentrate on the job of getting rid of the body."

"My truck," offered Jem. "Body away," he added. "Country."

Lady Severn said, "Yes, or there's the cellar here. We could bury him. Lanterns and things."

Virginius stopped himself in time from suggesting they ship Sid Fourpenny's body to some distant part of the world; he could see himself being sent out to get a large empty box.

He muttered, "Too expensive."

"I have an idea," Jean Quin said. "An excellent idea. It would be good theater and might do the Cause a lot of good."

Lady Severn: "Let's hear it, dear."

Jean told her idea. The others offered her muted congratulations. "Thank you," she said. "It's nothing really."

"And tomorrow?" asked Virginius.

Madge said, "To be perfectly honest, I do not think much of Mr. Fourpenny's idea. Though may he rest in peace. It seems to backfire."

"Then why not do as first proposed. One of you women faint, and one of us'll shoot the Chancellor."

"Fine. Who will do the shooting?"

"Handle that," Jem said.

It was dark out. The homeward rush of traffic was over.

The streets were quiet. All was serenity apart from the inner man of Virginius Twyce.

Nibbling a lip which, tender with past abuse, was already oozing blood, Virginius crept along the pavement, pushing Sid Fourpenny's motor-assisted bicycle. His knees were trembling, his stomach was contracted with fear. Had he had the emotion to spare, he would have railed loudly at the injustice of it all. Why was he always the one who had to do the dirty work, handle the most difficult, dangerous tasks? As it was, he could only fight his fear, willing himself to stay with the machine until he had taken it a safe distance from Lady Severn's.

He crossed a junction quickly, darting glances, wincing at the ticking noise given out by the bike's wheels. At any moment he was expecting to hear a stern voice calling on him to halt in the name of the law. He would be gripped on the shoulder by a burly policeman and questioned.

"Where do you think you're going with that motor-assisted bicycle?"

"W-walking."

"Whose is it?"

"Mine, officer."

"Let me see your ownership papers, insurance, and driving license."

"I, er, don't seem to have them with me."

The shoulder grip tightens, the voice becomes gritty. "It's not your motor-assisted bicycle at all, is it?"

"Not actually, no, I—"

"Where's the man who owns it? What have you *done* with him?"

Virginius spat out a mouthful of blood, wrenched the picture from his mind, and trembled on. He passed a couple cuddled together in a doorway, and as he passed, their talk ceased. It was easy enough for him to guess what they were thinking: *That's odd; a man pushing a bicycle. Why isn't he riding it? He's just stolen it, you can tell. We should overpower him. We should shout for help.*

Virginius gave up. His nerves could take no more. Besides,

surely he was far enough now from Lady Severn's. Turning into a side street, he let the machine loose and took to his heels, almost shrieking at the crash of the falling bike.

He ran until exhaustion impelled him to stop. Gasping, mopping at sweat, he sat on a doorstep. There were no sounds of chase. His trembling stopped, and with full recovery came satisfaction. He had done it; he had succeeded. The tough part was over. Now came the facile job of stealing a car.

Virginius got up and strode confidently away.

The suburban business section was suitably deserted, the street lighting dim, the shops all long since closed for the night. A depressed-looking cat was the sole observer when a vehicle with a commercial back and the front of a Rolls Royce tooled slowly along the street and came to a halt before one of the shops. Jem Gate got out of his truck.

In the shopwindow was displayed a photograph of a hearse, that and nothing else. A neon sign said twitchingly, "24 HOUR SERVICE."

Jem tried the door. It was unlocked. He entered, accompanied by the first four notes of "Abide With Me." In the light from the neon he saw that he was in a room with a pair of coffins on either side, more photographs of hearses, and a calendar.

A man appeared. He was short, hunched, old, and peery. He said, "She's gone then?"

Jem grunted.

"Accept the condolences of Bell and Son," the old man said threateningly.

"All right."

"If you'll step into the office, we'll fix it up."

Jem tapped the nearest coffin. "How much?"

"That thing? Fifteen quid. Not worth a damn. She'll be through it in no time. I've got you something better. Don't argue. Step in."

The old man retreated to an inner room. Jem took from

his wallet fifteen pounds, which he put on one of the coffins. He picked up his choice. It was as light as cardboard. He thought compassionately of Virginius Twyce.

Outside, Jem put the coffin on the back of his truck, got behind the wheel, and drove off. He mused that this lark was costing him a packet. He would be glad when it was all over

"Careful," Lady Severn said tightly. "Let me go first."

"We'll be all right if you just keep a firm grip," Jean Quin panted.

Madge and Jean were at the top of the flight of stairs which went down to the entrance hall of the house. Between them hung the late Sid Fourpenny. Each woman had an arm around her shoulders, its hand clasped in both of hers. By pulling down mightily on the hand and keeping close in, they managed to keep their burden almost to its true height.

The body's head was swathed in a toothache scarf and topped by a Severn hat which, stripped of its adornments, looked sufficiently masculine, if one ignored the material, shiny rafia, and the color: pink. There was nothing they could do about the lolling of the head or the trailing of the feet, but in all other respects they considered their efforts first-class.

Without removing Mr. Fourpenny's clothing they had searched through it to find and cut away all laundry marks and trade labels, they had emptied the pockets, they had shaved off the mustache, and Jean had worked on the face with cosmetics "to make him look more real," while Madge had written out the card which was to be delivered with the body.

"We're doing fine," Lady Severn gasped.

"Huh," grunted Jean, who was selflessly taking most of the weight.

The staircase was wide enough for their close three-abreast. They went down a step at a time, every thud of female shoes being followed by the drag-clump of male toe-caps, then the older woman's, "Sshh."

They reached the level, at which moment the front door opened, and a man came in.

Jean Quin was not in the least surprised. She had seen this bit a hundred times in movies, and someone always came in. Had no one come in she would have felt uncomfortable.

"Oh, dear," Lady Severn said, throwing the man a sheepish smile.

Jean laughed in a merry way. "Poor old Robert. That party was too much for him, I fear."

"Indeed, indeed," Madge stammered.

"He is as tight as a tick, is our friend Robert Jones, aged forty."

"Yes, poor old Robert Jones."

"From Bristol."

"He certainly is."

The man walked past them without a glance and trotted briskly up.

Sulky at being ignored, Jean called, "It was a good party, wasn't it, Margeret?"

"Yes, Jennifer."

"Yes.

"Very."

"But it will be grand to get back home to Scotland."

"Very grand, Marjorie."

The footsteps above faded and died.

"Oh, well done," Lady Severn whispered. "That was a magnificent performance."

Jean sniffed. "Thank you. I didn't have my hands free, and my movements were restricted, but under the circumstances I don't suppose I did too badly."

"Magnificent, dear, magnificent. I feel privileged."

Both glowing cheerily, they turned and struggled on to the rear of the house. They had only a minute to wait outside before the arrival of Mr. Gate. Jean took the scarf and hat. Jem laid the body out in the coffin and placed on top Lady Severn's card, which read, "I am the corpse of British theater."

Jem got back behind the wheel. "Night."

"Good luck," Jean said. "Don't be late for the do tomorrow."

"Good-bye, Mr. Gate," said Lady Severn "Good-bye, Mr. Fourpenny."

Striding along, humming a tune, Virginius thought, as he had on previous occasions, that it was the really simple things that proved the most difficult. Here he was, after half an hour's searching, still without a car. It was amusing, really. Who would have imagined that all the dozens of parked cars examined not only didn't have the keys in their ignitions but were locked to boot.

Now Virginius came onto a wide road and saw what he wanted, what he had expected to find long ago. The car, standing in front of a theater, had its driver's door open, its lights on, and its engine running.

Virginius sauntered across, circled the car to make sure the tires were in decent condition, got in, and drove unhurriedly off.

When he reached the meeting place, Trafalgar Square, Jem Gate had already arrived. The car was not wide enough to take all the coffin; a foot of it stuck out; the door couldn't be closed. Virginius said he hadn't far to go; he didn't suppose anyone would notice.

"Night, all," Jem said.

Driving off, Virginius saw that the fuel gauge showed the tank to be low. He tutted with annoyance. What if he'd needed to go a long way? It would have been awkward, for he had no money with him to buy petrol. He shuddered, thinking of the embarrassment of going into a service station and trying to cadge a couple of gallons.

He came to Whitehall, turned into Downing Street. There were one or two stragglers, one or two policemen.

Virginius stopped in front of Number 11. A constable trotted up and fully opened the open door, saluting. Virginius, being ignored as a mere chauffeur, got out and walked away. As he neared the steps going down into St. James's Park, he heard the officer ask, "Are you feeling unwell, sir?"

six

Jean Quin bustled around her flat. If she didn't hurry, if she didn't manage to get a cab as soon as she hit the street, she would be late in meeting the others at the rally grounds, which was of no great consequence except that they might be panicked into rash acts if she didn't turn up in time with the gun.

Last night Jean had persuaded her colleagues that it would be safer were she herself to transport the weapon to Kent: You never knew; there might be a search of males at the entrance. She won her case. She won because she had to win. Her arrangement would be ruined if she had no gun to give Starchmount.

Jean was sped into faster bustling by the thoughts of her friends acting on their own, scaring the Chancellor into a hiding in which he could never be gotten at, or of Montague Starchmount assuming she was not coming and returning to Downing Street.

At last she was ready. Pulling a gun-moll, Ida Lupino-ish mouth, she got the revolver from under her pillow and rootled it to the bottom of her bag.

The doorbell rang.

Oh, no, thought Jean. Bloody no.

She strode to the door, yanked it open, and was faced by the first of her lovers from Number 11, Green-Jones, who frowned a cheery greeting as he walked inside and said, "You'll be thrilled to know, Ninotchka, that I have a free morning. The boss has gone to a do in Kent."

"Lovely," Jean said, following him into the living room and pulling on the tail of his coat. "But I'm engaged."

"May I offer my felicitations?"

Jean tugged hard. "No."

Green-Jones gave in to the tug by slipping off his coat. "All right, we'll get straight at it." He grabbed Jean's arm. "To the bedroom."

There was a steady blare of noise. Mainly it was music. This you could tell from the record players that were in use or, if you were brave enough of eardrum, by standing close to one of the hundred-odd loudspeakers, each of which was perversely giving out a different tune. There were no winners. The battle was augmented by the crash of equipment from the rides, the shouts of spielers, the crowd's babble, and the steady drone from the gossiping politicians, each of whom was purposely saying something different and listening to the music of his own blare while thinking that what the other man made was mainly noise.

Jem Gate strolled around, his stub hands clasped behind. He was in cheerful, relaxed spirits. The situation he felt as good; felt it would work itself out to his full satisfaction. On the morrow, he told himself, there would be a return to normal routine. He would be a different man, of course, changed by his experience. But he would be a better man.

Jem wandered on among the attractions, there being a little time to kill. He listened with earnest face to the spielers, resisted the draw of a beer tent, and stood, wearing an externally avuncular smile, by a fun house to watch girls' skirts blowing up and their hands fighting each other to not prevent their skirts from blowing up. He was having a grand time.

Turning away, his gaze fell on a booth covered with rosettes and topped by a sign urging one and all to join the

Young Liberals without delay. Jem stopped. He sobered. His eyes became wistful.

A female within the booth smiled at him encouragingly and reminded him of the danger. He walked on, tightening the muscles of his neck with determination.

"What passion," Green-Jones murmured, fleetingly exchanging his look of nastiness for one of bewilderment. "What speed."

Right, Jean thought, the fastest act of love on record. She leaped from the bed and began to fight her way into her clothes.

Naked except for his shoes, Green-Jones sat up and asked, "What are you doing? I've got all morning."

"Bathroom."

"With all your clothes on?"

"Doctor's orders," Jean spat, yanking up a zip. "I've got a cold."

The doorbell rang.

With a gag of panic, not daring to look at her watch, Jean grabbed her bag and the rest of her clothes and ran out of the room. "Don't move!" she yelled, closing him in.

She opened the front door. The visitor was Mr. Percival. He bundled inside, explaining that he had a free morning because the Chancellor had gone to a rally.

"Darling," he went on, dropping onto the couch, "I shall read you chapters Nine, Ten, and Eleven, with short breaks between to satisfy your passion for me."

"Divine," Jean groaned.

"Let me help." He jumped up and dragged off the jacket Jean was struggling to get on.

In the carnival's center was a space the size of a tennis court. It was much as described by Mrs. Quin. At one side stood a long table draped in flags. Behind, on the tent the table was backed up against, were hung propaganda posters. On that side of the table spread a group of men wearing rosettes and clamped-on smiles and marvelous haircuts. On the front side, one at each corner, stood two large men with folded arms, bowler hats, and bleak faces.

Lady Severn was examining these two anomalies while waiting for the signal to faint. She thought they looked grim enough, resolute enough, to be public relations officers.

In festive mood today, despite still secretly mourning the death of Sid Fourpenny, Madge wore a cartwheel hat covered with tulle of a strong purple, which she thought went nicely with the occasional flecks of mauve in her tweed suit. She also wore long black gloves and carried a shooting stick.

There were twenty or thirty people standing or turgidly milling in the center space. Threading between, Lady Severn reached the table's right-hand corner, which she decided would be her stage. She examined the scattered crowd. On the edge stood Virginius Twyce, pretending to read a pamphlet. Coming into view from the backs of stalls was Jem Gate. There was no sign of Mrs. Quin.

Lady Severn hoped Jean wouldn't be late. Without her, or rather the gun, nothing could be accomplished. But perhaps she had already arrived and had given the gun to Mr. Gate. So thinking, Madge looked back at the sculptor.

Jem Gate, near the front of the crowd now, caught her eye and nodded.

That's it, thought Lady Severn. The signal.

She flung up her arms and, with a cry of "I'm fainting," keeled over onto the grass.

Mr. Percival got off the couch and reached for his briefcase. "Now for Chapter Nine."

Jean followed off the couch and staggered toward her clothes. She squealed when the doorbell rang.

"What's wrong?" jerked the biographer.

"Quick, quick!" Jean gabbled, pushing him into the kitchen. "It's my mother."

She stumbled back to her clothes, bundled them up before her, and fell into the hall, shouting, "Go away!"

A fist pounded on the wood. The knock was too authoritative to deny.

Jean opened the door a crack. The caller was Mr. Crippenson. He raised his hat.

Jean said, "You've come because the Chancellor's gone to Kent."

"No, I've come because I've just broken off my engagement. I'm all yours."

"No!"

Crippenson pushed inside. Moaning, Jean let her arms and knees sag. Assisting her the rest of the way down, Crippenson said, "Yes, here's as good as anywhere."

Virginius Twyce, who had been approaching Lady Severn to have a conspiratorial word, drew back in twittering alarm at her faint. His alarm swiftly turned to embarrassment, both for Lady Severn and himself—what if people realized he and she were together? Swinging about, he charged through the crowd in a bent-legged crouch, his shoulders high.

He left the space, circled a tent, and returned at his normal height and wearing a different expression. Standing in a mild sweat at the crowd's rear, he watched Lady Severn being half carried away by two fat, middle-aged women in nurse uniform who were burned crimson with excitement.

The drama ended, Virginius gave his attention back to what he had intended asking Lady Severn about: the anomalous pair at the table ends. He didn't like the looks of them at all.

Musing that there would be no harm in asking someone else, he chose the man at his side. The man wore an ankle-length black coat, a deerstalker cap, and a monocle. He had silver hair and the face of a well-starved horse.

"Excuse me, sir," Virginius said. "Could you inform me as to the identity of those two gentlemen in bowler hats?"

The man nodded royally. "A pleasure, sir. They are armed bodyguards from Scotland Yard."

"Oh, bother."

"I agree. But after last night's debacle, it was felt they were necessary."

"What happened last night?"

"It's in the paper. Here, I have finished with it." The man handed over the *Times* with all the pomp of an emissary delivering a papal bull which annulled a millionaire's stale marriage.

Virginius took the paper and began to read the headline story. It concerned the finding outside 11 Downing Street of the body of a murdered man who had been identified by a tattoo as being one Sidney Fourpenny of Enfield. He was known to be a Socio-Demo-Fascinist. Many SDF's had been arrested, and the others were being sought. The police commissioner had promoted the constable, whose work had led to the finding of the body.

"Not," said the man with the monocle, "that it has deterred the Chancellor. When the trumpet sounds, he will appear to make his speech."

"Good."

"I could not agree more."

Jean rolled the limp, panting Mr. Crippenson to one side of the hall and rolled herself over onto her hands and knees. She crawled to the telephone, dialed, and asked feebly for a cab to come at once.

"Are we going somewhere, dear?" whispered Mr. Crippenson.

"Belt up," returned Jean in a weak snarl. Ignoring her underclothes, she dragged on skirt, blouse, and jacket.

The doorbell rang.

Springing to life Jean ripped upright the startled Mr. Crippenson, bundled him into the bathroom, and told him she would stick a knife in his heart if he made a sound. Snatching up her bag with determination, she stomped to the door. She had had enough of this farce, which she had seen a dozen times under various names. With her it wasn't funny.

She flung open the door and snapped, "Buzz off, Hobbset."

The visitor was not Hobbset, the leakage expert. It was Molly, the cook.

Face twitching with fury, Molly put a hand on Jean's chest and propelled her backward into the living room. Molly had a cheated-wife look.

She said, "I want to know how long this rotten affair's been going on between you and the Chancellor."

"Me?"

"Yes, you. There's no good denying it, 'cos I've paid a pretty penny to Mr. Hobbset for the evidence, what takes the shape of letters."

"Good old Hobbset."

"Never mind him. We're on about you. You can just keep your filthy hands off the Chancellor, 'cos he's mine. See?"

The doorbell rang.

Jean charged to the door. It was a taxi driver. "Be right down," she said, and rushing back to the living room, yelled, "Come and get me, darling!" before leaving Molly frozen with gape and running out of the flat.

Standing stolidly at the front of the growing crowd, Jem Gate was wondering why Lady Severn, her hat awry and being watched narrow-eyed by two fat nurses, was giving him a pained stare. Her practice faint had been quite well done.

"Pssst!" said the voice of Virginius Twyce in his ear.

"Well?"

"Those two morons by the table are armed bodyguards. Read all about it."

A newspaper was pushed under Jem's arm. He unfolded it and read the headline story, tutting that there was no mention of the corpse of British theater and thinking how ridiculous of the authorities to connect Mr. Fourpenny with the Socio-Demo-Fascinists, despite what Twyce had said.

About to refold the newspaper, Jem's eye was caught by a familiar name. Open-mouthed, glaring belligerently at close range, he read how a certain Cuthbert "Dainty" Macklesfield had been arrested the previous night while trying to escape on foot from a theater he had robbed at gunpoint.

What rotten filthy lousy stinking putrid luck, Jem mentally gnashed. Him and his rotten television payment.

Furious, Jem swept the paper to the ground.

That's it! thought Lady Severn. The signal!

"I am fainting!" she yelled, and crashed down to the grass.

Forward rushed the two nurses. "Let's get her back to the tent, Mary!" one cried. "Roger, Agnes!" the other shouted. They grabbed an arm apiece and began to pull.

"No, no," Lady Severn snapped, kicking out. "Those men behind the table have got to help. I say, you men?"

The politicals looked on with professional smiles of sympathy while automatically breathing through their mouths; these smiles were generally used when talking to suffering miners who had BO.

"Come on, ducky, back to the first-aid tent," a nurse grated, wrenching Lady Severn to her feet.

"And this time," insisted the other, "you've *got* to have some hot tea. Right, Agnes?"

"Roger, Mary."

By the lack of commotion and gunfire Madge Severn realized that the signal had been another false alarm. She struggled fiercely. "Let bloody well go. I'm better now."

"Hysteria in patient," said one of the nurses. "Page thirty. Remember, Mary?"

"Roger, Agnes," the other said. She pulled Lady Severn's body over into the horizontal and got an armlock around her head.

Not able to see on account of her hat being over her face, Madge felt the fear of the unknown as she was dragged forward like a stage horse's rear end. Into her hat she shouted, "Negative negative!"

The fainting routine, Virginius Twyce thought, was not only horribly embarrassing but totally useless. The bodyguards had moved not a muscle. The time had come for a more positive action.

With a sigh bred almost of boredom, Virginius pushed his way through the growing crowd and went to front the nearest bodyguard. He asked, "Where can I find a policeman?"

The plainclothes officer looked him over carefully. "Why?"

"I've just heard some men talking about assassinating someone. They have a bomb."

"What!"

"I said I've just heard—"

"Where?" barked the bodyguard, leaning forward, grabbing Virginius by the lapel.

"Follow me."

Virginius led the way to the rim of the space and into a narrow gap between booths. He pointed to the canvas. "They're in there. Listen."

The man crouched close to the canvas wall. Virginius stepped back and looked around on the grass. He was not surprised to see that he had a choice of weapons—a mallet, several empty beer bottles, a tent stave. He chose a bottle.

When hit, the bodyguard sank without a sound. Virginius dropped his weapon and went in search of Mrs. Quin.

The taxi screeched to a stop. Jean Quin thrust money at the driver, plus the five pounds she had promised him if he would break the speed laws. She sprang from the cab, entered the grounds, stopped the first man she saw, and asked him if the Chancellor had made his speech yet.

"Who?" the man said.

Jean ran on, asked someone else. She learned that she was not too late. Groaning out a long sigh, she recovered her cool and went tenderly in search of Montague Starchmount, whose celibacy she thought was one of the nicest things that had ever happened to her.

She came to the center space. It was well filled with people. Here a family picnicked, there two drunks were singing in each other's faces, women sat knitting, and children dodged about.

Jean saw Montague Starchmount. Going across, she thought he looked rather cute in his black coat and deerstalker cap. She told him so.

"Thank you," he said. "Actually the garments constitute a disguise."

"Very good."

"And at the penultimate moment I shall remove my monocle."

"There's a brave man," Jean said, patting his arm. "Where's the Chancellor?"

"He will appear when the trumpet sounds."

"Then that's the time to do it."

"I agree."

"Not nervous?"

"Slightly, I must confess. Mainly because of two persons in bowler hats. One is momentarily absent. You observe the other?"

"I observe."

"They are armed bodyguards."

"I'll see what I can do to draw that one away. Here, Starchmount, take the gun."

"Thanks awfully."

Virginius Twyce reached for Mrs. Quin's arm and drew her to a stop. "I thought you'd never get here."

"I was delayed. It's quite a funny story."

"Oh?"

"Or painful. Depends how you feel about it."

"Never mind now," Virginius said. "Give me the gun, and I'll take it to Mr. Gate."

"Actually I was keeping this as a surprise, but I can see I'll have to tell you. The fact is, I've arranged for the assassination myself."

"Really? Good show."

"It's that monocled type behind you."

Virginius glanced back. "Ah, yes. He seems a nice chap."

"I hope Mr. Gate won't be too disappointed."

"So do I," Virginius said worriedly, scraping a lip with his teeth. "I'll go and tell him."

He sidled away, sidled through the crowd, and sidled up to the sculptor. "Psst," he said. "Sorry and all that, but Mrs. Quin has arranged for someone else to kill the Chancellor."

Mr. Gate, looking unhappily at the ground, merely shrugged.

Virginius gave his shoulder a sympathetic pat and sidled away.

A second after Mr. Twyce had left his bleak presence, another voice hissed in Jem's ear. It said, "Hey there, Mr. Gate."

"Whozat?"

"Me—Mel."

"Mel Macklesfield?" Jem asked, hardly daring to look around, hardly daring to hope.

"Right you are. See, our Dainty got himself lumbered doing a little job last night. It was in the papers."

"Saw it."

"Front page," Mel said proudly. "Not bad, eh?"

"Rotten business," Jem complained.

"Yeah, well, he would've been all right if some thieving bastard hadn't stolen his car."

"What about job?"

"Oh, that's all right, Mr. Gate. Don't you fret about that. The Macklesfields don't let no one down. *I'll* do it."

Jem brightened. He took a deep breath. "You will?"

"Absolutely. I've brought me own shooter, and I'm ready for action."

"Good, good," Jem said. "Good."

"Now where is your Intended, Mr. Gate?"

"Not here," Jem said. "Listen." He gave Mel a rough description. "Here soon."

"I'm ready. You just tell me when."

Jean Quin thought that if she took care of the present

bodyguard, Lady Severn would surely take care of the other when he reappeared. However, Jean decided against fainting. Two fainters at the same time was a bit much. She would stick to the tried and true.

Through the front of the crowd she stared at the bodyguard until she caught his eye. She winked. He blinked. She winked again. His face lost its severity. To the third wink she added a small, sexy smile. He swallowed. With the fourth wink she tilted her head to the side and then began to stroll away in that direction. The bodyguard followed.

Jean led the way to a secluded spot between booths. She turned, smiling. The bodyguard came up close. He was not smiling. "Okay," he said harshly, "what's with this corny come-hither bit?"

"Ah," said Jean, seeing that this time sex was a failure. "I—um—have a grave matter to report."

"Like what?"

"Like a plot."

"Eh?"

"Yes, to kill the Chancellor."

The bodyguard managed to look both shocked and delighted. "Where?" he asked. "Who?"

"It's a secret organization."

"The Socio-Demo-Fascinists!"

"Right," said Jean happily. "Come closer, and I'll tell you all the details."

"Yes, yes." The bodyguard took a step forward.

Jean kicked him on the shin.

With a strangled yelp the man bent over, grabbing for his leg. Jean looked around, saw part of a tent pole, picked it up, and gave the bodyguard a mighty blow on the head. He dropped.

The loudspeakers of the inner space crackled, rang, coughed, and started to give out a trumpet voluntary.

Lady Severn, in the first-aid tent, struggled to get away from her two captors, Virginius Twyce pressed forward eagerly, Mel Macklesfield watched the man at his side, waiting for the word, Jean Quin left the unconscious bodyguard and ran from the booths, and Montague Starchmount took out his monocle.

The Chancellor of the Exchequer was a lean man. He looked tired. He also looked nervous. A muscle was twitching under his left eye.

Cutting short the politician who was making an elaborate introduction, he stepped to the microphone himself. After giving his twitching muscle a pat of reassurance, he said, "Ladies and gentlemen, dear friends, I speak to you today as a man who has seen the light. In response to the thousands of letters of protest I have received, I have decided to take off the newly imposed tax on theater seats."

Virginius Twyce, surprised, stared at the Chancellor, who was still speaking. Jean Quin gagged, gasped, turned from her place at the edge of the crowd, and went to find and restrain Starchmount.

Jem Gate smiled. He fell into a reverie. He thought it was rather nice that there was no need now for anyone to kill the Chancellor, which, even before, had been a ridiculous idea, one with which he would have had nothing to do himself. Fancy wanting to kill the poor man. But the other killing, the one he had spent so much time on in looking for a professional murderer, had to be gone through with. It was the only way. Then the coast would be clear. Lady Severn, dear Lady Severn, would have no more disappointments. Not that she'd had any since he had joined the Group, only previously, in her pre-London life. There had, though, been some close shaves lately.

Tony Zero, to begin with. By stalking out of the flat that day he had shown himself to be a potential disappointer. Obviously he did not have the kindness to even pretend going along with Lady Severn's plan. True, he had not really caused her any pain, not yet, but it was certain he was going to. The only way to protect Lady Severn was by killing Tony. Which had been simple enough. The knife went in with the greatest of ease.

Pat Single was another one who came close to being a disappointment to the head and founder of Bloomsbury Group Junior. It was clear from the way she acted in Hyde Park that she was going to do something which would sorely try Lady Severn, who, fortunately, was too sweet and innocent to see the coming danger. But *he* saw it and acted accordingly. Patricia was stopped in time. Being without suspicion, as well as small, it was no trouble to strangle her. And typing the suicide note had been pretty smart, wrapping up the two killings as nice as you please. Lady Severn had been sad, yes, but she had been saved from the suffering that would have come from the loss or treachery of a friend.

In the first-aid tent, the two nurses were putting up a stiff battle to contain their patient. Lady Severn, who had heard nothing of the Chancellor's speech, thought as she struck out with a straight left that at all costs she must get back to the crowd and help her friends. Perhaps things had gone wrong, in which case she would try to kill the Beast of Britain herself.

Following the left with a short right, Lady Severn broke free. She dashed for the door, tripped on a pile of bandages, and fell.

With the Chancellor's continuing speech coming faintly to his ears, Jem Gate was still in his reverie about his achievements in protecting the gentle feelings of his greatest friend, Lady Severn. It was too bad, he mused, that he'd had to electrocute poor old Relentable Cease. He had seemed a decent, inoffensive soul. However, it would have been very unhappy-making if he'd gone to the authorities with his message from the spirit of Pat Single about being strangled.

That nonsense, Jem admitted, had been his own fault, for he it was who had pushed the upturned glass around the circle. What else could he do? Lady Severn had looked so hurt when no spirits answered her greeting, and he wouldn't allow even the smallest hurt to touch his friend. He could have stopped there, of course, but it was hard to stop once started, it was hard to resist a bit of brag about how well he had done in killing Pat and faking the suicide note. The artist will have his recognition, his communication, one way or another.

That Minerva Droplet, Jem thought on, she came closest to causing deep disappointment, with her intention of going to the police with the story that Sid Fourpenny was a sex maniac and had killed Pat Single, which would have brought the whole Group under investigation. Luckily, after Lady Severn had telephoned word of the intention, though saying, in her innocence, that she didn't believe Minerva would really do it, Miss Droplet had not been too difficult to find. It was simply a matter of waiting outside the nearest police station to the Bloomsbury flat. When she wandered past, daydreaming, all he had to do was follow and wait for the right moment. Pushing her under the bus had been no problem at all. Again he had kept Lady Severn from being wounded by a friend's actions.

"Listen to me," Jean Quin hissed urgently, gripping Montague Starchmount's arm with both hands. "You've got to *listen.*"

The man in the deerstalker hat prized at her fingers. "Calmness, my dear. Everything is all right."

"It's not all right. I mean, yes, it is."

"There you are, you see."

"What I mean, for Christ's sake, is that everything's all right as far as the Chancellor's concerned."

"Yes, he makes a jolly decent target."

"No, no, you clot, I meant there's no need to kill him. It's all off. It's okay. No bang-bang. Shooting is out. Get me?"

"You are distraught."

"Damn right I am. Give me that gun."

"But *I* have a steady head. I never crack under strain. You just watch me."

"Listen!"

Starchmount freed his arm of the gripping fingers. "You have delayed me long enough. I am looking forward to this."

Jean tried to get at the gun in his pocket. "Gimme!"

Starchmount turned her around and gave her a friendly but firm shove. Jean went sprawling into the crowd.

Sid Fourpenny, Jem was thinking, might not have come to any dangerous conclusions in—as he reported to Lady Severn when telling of Droplet's death—his investigation into "something curious like," meaning of course the deaths of the others. It was better, however, to be on the safe side, to make certain that Sid could not cause Lady Severn to be disillusioned. Taking the safety catch off the gun was simplicity itself, although there had been a few anxious moments when the others started to handle the gun. . . .

Now there was just one killing to go.

"Furthermore," said the Chancellor of the Exchequer, his voice booming around through the loudspeakers, "the revenue which would have come from the tax on theater seats can be raised from a tax in other areas. For instance, there's children's orange juice, and . . ."

Virginius Twyce, listening to the speech, was beginning to wonder worriedly what he would do if the Chancellor were to put a tax on collectors of silver, when a movement in the corner of his eye caused him to turn his head and find thereupon a worry of far greater proportions.

The man in the deerstalker hat, gun in hand, was pushing through to the front of the crowd.

Virginius leaped from his place, ran along in front of the table, broke through the front rank of people, and met Starchmount, on whom he flung himself. They fell to the ground and rolled over, wrestling, moving away from the front and deeper into the crowd.

The Chancellor, after a muscle-twitching pause at the flurry of movement, went gamely on with his speech. Jem Gate listened placidly, waiting for the moment to order his assassin into action. Lady Severn, in the first-aid tent, was biting the hand that was trying to feed her a pill.

Montague Starchmount and Virginius Twyce rolled over and over. They punched and slapped and grappled. The surrounding people moved helpfully out of the way and watched with interest

"Desist!" snarled Starchmount.

"It's all off!" gasped Virginius.

He got himself on top of the other man, pinned his arms, and said, "Listen, listen, listen, I can explain."

Virginius had no chance to explain. At that moment onto the scene came blundering the bodyguard he had previously knocked out. The grim-faced man threw himself onto Virginius, and they both rolled over.

"Where's the bomb?" the bodyguard shouted.

"Don't let him get away," shouted Virginius. "He's going to kill—" A mouthful of grass gagged the rest.

Montague Starchmount, freed, got unsteadily up, murmuring his thanks to the man who had hauled off the mad attacker and looking around for his gun. He saw it, went to it, bent down to get it.

Jean Quin, who after being pushed by her celibate lover had found some difficulty in freeing herself from the people into whom she had staggered, now charged forward and took a great leap in the air.

She landed on Starchmount's back, he fell on his face, she grabbed him around the neck.

The second bodyguard, the one Jean had knocked out with a tent pole, came lurching through the crowd, a hand held to the bloody lump on his head. He saw the woman he wanted. She was sitting on the back of a man who was on his hands and knees.

The bodyguard grabbed Jean and pulled her up. "Got you!"

Jean gabbled, "Stop him! He's going to shoot the—"

The bodyguard cut her off with a hand on her throat. He hissed. "Not so loud—the Chancellor is speaking."

Montague Starchmount got groggily to his feet. He

straightened his clothes, looked at the two pairs of struggling people, cocked his gun, and headed for the Chancellor.

Virginius brought up his knee. The bodyguard gave a shriek and rolled aside. Virginius leaped up. He took a short run forward and flung himself into a horizontal dive at the retreating form of the man who had lost his deerstalker hat.

He hit Starchmount at knee level and clung tight. Starchmount fell flat on his face. Virginius crawled up his back and sat on his shoulders. He reached for the gun in the other's hand.

Into the arena strode a short man with no neck: Commander Salem of the SDF, in mufti. He was on the run from the police because of the murder of his new cousin, Sid Fourpenny. Obviously the man responsible for it was this one, who had spied on Sid outside GHQ.

Commander Salem threw himself viciously on Virginius Twyce.

They rolled over and rolled into the first bodyguard, who was recovering from the kick in the groin. He grabbed each man around the neck and began to pound their heads together.

Jean Quin and the other bodyguard were kicking at each other's legs.

Montague Starchmount got shatteredly to his feet. A glazed glance around told him there would be no more interruptions; everyone seemed to be occupied. He took a firm grip on the gun and loped toward the front of the crowd.

"What?" snapped Jem Gate in a loud voice. He was no longer listening placidly. His face was white with shock.

The Chancellor of the Exchequer looked twitchingly at the heckler. "Eh?"

"Tax what?"

"Well, wheelchairs and—"

"Before that."

"Oh, marble. Imported marble. I put a tax on it this morning."

Jem was outraged. He was about to charge when in front

of him appeared a man in a long black coat, a man who was raising a gun, a man who must be Jean Quin's assassin. But this was no longer political. This was personal.

Jem stepped forward. He wrenched the gun from the hand of Jean's man, leaned over the table, pointed the weapon at the startled multi-twitching face of the Chancellor of the Exchequer, and fired.

Instantly all was chaos. People and officials pushed, screamed, yelled orders, fell flat, ran, grabbed one another.

Jem Gate found himself under the table. At once he was joined by Mel Macklesfield, who said, shouting to make himself heard above the bedlam, "What you want to go and do that for?"

"Annoyed me," Jem said, throwing his gun aside. "Come on."

He began to crawl along under the table. Mel moved at his shoulder, saying, "Anyway, didn't you tell me awhile back that your Intended was a woman?"

"Yes. Come on."

"The job's still on then?"

"Yes."

They reached the end of the table. Jem lifted the flap of flags. Coming from the first-aid tent, following two nurses who were running with a stretcher, was Lady Severn, her hat on one side, her clothes awry.

"There," Jem said. "Big hat."

"Got you."

"Make it quick."

"Right."

They got out from under the table. Mel slipped away, Jem turned from the bedlam and went between two stalls. He knew exactly where to find that booth covered with rosettes.

A gunshot sounded. Jem smiled, sadly yet with satisfaction. That was one killing he could never have brought himself to do. Now there would be no more disappointments for Lady Severn. Certainly not the biggest disappointment of all. She was safe. She would never be shocked and wounded to the core of her gentle soul by knowing what he had made up his mind to do at the first emergency meeting but couldn't do until he had arranged for her death and what he was going to do right now: join the Young Liberals.

"The Chancellor is dead," crackled a voice from the loudspeakers. "Long live the Chancellor."

Lady Severn looked up brightly at the boomed information. Flushing with pleasure, she stepped back from the pile of struggling bodies at her feet—the two nurses, a policeman, three politician's wives, and a boy scout—who had flung themselves on the man with the pistol (a horrid crook, no doubt, out to rob someone) after Lady Severn, furious with him for firing off his gun near at hand, had felled him neatly with a blow from her shooting stick.

She stood back, forgot the struggling pile and the greater chaos beyond, turned away. Success, she thought, wonderful lovely success. A triumph for the Group, which now though would have to be disbanded for safety's sake. It was, in any case, rather depleted. But there would be other Groups, more dear, kind, decent friends. She would leave at once, for New York. A lot of lovely work to be done there. All those foolish, misguided delegates to the United Nations, they needed to be put out of the way for the safety of the world. And then there were Europe's various royal families to be dealt with. And then that silly party in Moscow. And then . . .

Lady Severn straightened her hat, hummed a snatch of tune, and ' rolled toward the exit, swinging her shooting stick.

"Long live the Chancellor."